ALWAYS

- AND -

FOREVER

THE CHAOS STATION STORIES

JENN BURKE

KELLY JENSEN

ALWAYS AND FOREVER

ISBN-13: 9781541018822

GRADUATION

REUNION

KISS THE GUARDIAN

SALUTE TO THE SUN

HONEYMOON

Second Edition, February 2017

Collected here are the extra stories Jenn and I wrote alongside the Chaos Station series. "Graduation" and "Reunion" are set before the adventure begins, "Kiss the Guardian" and "Salute to the Sun" during the action, and "Honeymoon" serves as our epilogue.

Because so many of our readers expressed an interest in having a piece of Chaos Station—and maybe because we also wanted something for our bookshelves—we decided to make this collection of stories available in print.

So this is for you, our readers. Thank you for taking this journey with us, and thank you for loving our boys as much as we do.

Best,
Kelly & Jenn

GRADUATION 7

REUNION.. 53

KISS THE GUARDIAN 91

SALUTE TO THE SUN... 99

HONEYMOON.. 119

EXTRAS 169

    Snakes on a Ship 171

    Therapy... 177

    Interview with AllSpace Alliance News........... 187

    Chaos Station by the Numbers....................... 195

GRADUATION

In *Chaos Station* (Chaos Station #1), Zander Anatolius and Felix Ingesson are reunited after nine years apart. Zander believes Felix was captured and executed by the enemy in the years long Human-Stin War. Felix believes Zander was swallowed by a black ops program, probably never to surface again. Their reunion, therefore, is a rather profound event and the basis for the five-book Chaos Station series.

That's not where their story begins, however.

Zander was Felix's first love. They met when they were eight years old and, after ten years of friendship, Felix confessed his feelings to Zander on the night they were to graduate Shepard Academy (military school). They'd be hopping on different shuttles the next day as each pursued a separate career within the Allied Earth Forces.

Why did Felix wait so long? Because first love can be overwhelming and terrifying—and because he was fairly certain his feelings were one sided. He knew Zander loved him as a friend and didn't think he could expect more. He was wrong. His confession prompted Zander to examine his own feelings. Zander quickly came to the realization that what he and Felix shared was more than simple friendship, but it was too late to explore further.

So they decided to share just one night—and that was all they had for four years. "Graduation" is the story of that night.

The story of Zander and Felix continues through several more shorts and the five novels of the Chaos Station series. You can read and download the shorts for free at our website, http://chaosstation.com, where you will also find excerpts, cut scenes and the first chapter of every book.

We hope you enjoy this introduction to Zander and Felix!

Happy reading,
Kelly & Jenn

Chapter One

Earth, 2256

Eyeing the trousers hanging over the back of the chair, Felix caught a fold of fabric between thumb and forefinger and rubbed experimentally. Soft, really soft. He could barely feel the embedded smart fiber that would prevent wear and tear. Edging his thumb toward the outside of the leg, he looked for a seam and discovered it was one of the turned in kind he couldn't pick at. He'd have to do something else with his hands if he wore these trousers to the graduation party. No pockets, either. Who the fuck wore pants with no pockets?

Zed would, and he'd look tall, dark and handsome. Next to him, Felix would look scrawny. And with his blond curls, wide hazel eyes, delicate nose and full mouth he would always look boyish. He could really use a good scar or something.

The door to his quarters clicked softly. Clad only in a towel from a recent trip to the shower, Felix backed into the corner and assumed a defensive posture—arms raised, weight balanced on the balls of his feet. It was late in the day for a last minute prank, but he wouldn't put it past someone to try. The door swished open and a familiar shadow slipped inside the room.

Felix dropped his stance. "How the fuck did you hack the code? It took me twenty-four Standard hours to write that one."

Marnie held up her wallet and grinned. The holo playing above the fold flashed off her exotic features, lighting her dark eyes and making the line of her bangs more severe. "You based it on the same sequence you used for the janitorial closet in second year."

"I turned that code inside out."

"Not enough times."

"Damn it."

She reached up to ruffle his damp curls. "There, there. If you'd used an old fashioned padlock, I'd have been stumped." Marnie couldn't pick anything "dumb" to save her life. She was resourceful, though.

Ducking out of her reach, Felix smacked a wall panel and reached inside his closet for underwear and socks. He dropped his towel and donned both while Marnie stared through him. He wasn't offended by her lack of interest in his private parts. Girls didn't do it for him and he didn't do it for Marnie. She and Ryan had hooked up the year before and, by all measures, were set to be partnered for life. But he did recognize the blankness of her expression.

"Stop thinking so hard," he said. "You'll short something in your perfect brain."

"How would you get around a padlock if you didn't have any tools on hand?" she asked.

"I'd go find some tools."

"Say you can't, just for the sake of this exercise." Marnie always did shit like this—asked him to think. Mostly, Felix enjoyed it.

"I'd try force, first," he said. "A kick to the mechanism. Then I'd go look for some tools."

"But what if—"

"We're going to be late for the party if you keep what-ifing. What are you doing here, anyway?"

She was already dressed in something long, flowy and purple. She looked good, if not exactly Marnie-like. He was used to seeing her in uniform.

"I brought you something." Marnie held up a shirt. More grey fabric, but less dark than the trousers, and sort of shiny. It looked like one of Zed's shirts. All swank and soft and costly. Felix chewed on his lips, a habit he'd formed to give himself time to think before he blurted out the first words that came to mind.

"I know gifts embarrass you, Flick"—his friends all called him by the same nickname his sister had given him when she was a toddler. Sometimes it made him self-conscious, but usually it made him feel as if he was with family—"but I also know how important tonight is and I wanted you to feel good about what you were wearing. Zed's going to take one look—"

"I was thinking I'd just wear my uniform." Felix was stupidly proud of the new ribbons on the breast pocket, even though he knew they would mean absolutely nothing after today. He'd no longer be a student who had excelled, despite humble beginnings—top of his class in five out of eight disciplines. He'd be a raw cadet on his way to specialist training.

And he'd be alone.

Marnie's brows disappeared into her bangs. "What? No, you can't do that. We're all getting dressed up."

Felix reached into the closet for his uniform pants and pulled them on, buying some more time to think. "And I don't think I'm going to say anything to Zed."

"Don't make me kick your ass."

"What good will it do? This is the last time I'm going to see him for months. Maybe even years. Or ever." Felix's heart thumped up and down hard enough to bruise all attending parts. "Besides, he and Emma make a good couple."

"Zed isn't in love with Emma."

"You don't need to be in love with someone to…" Felix let the rest of his statement fizzle on his tongue. He knew Zed wasn't in love with Emma, despite the fact they had everything in common, including a career path that would take them to specialist training together.

"I swear, Felix." He really did prefer Flick. "If you don't tell Zed how you feel tonight, I'll do it for you."

All of his blood rushed to his socked feet. "You wouldn't."

"Don't try me."

"Marnie…"

"And no whining, it doesn't suit you."

Irritated, Felix reached for his shirt.

Marnie yanked it from his hands. "It will be too late tomorrow. Do you really want to go through life with that what-if unanswered?"

"He's my best friend. That's enough."

Cuddling both his uniform shirt and the new one to her chest, she shook her head. "No, it's not. I can see it in your face every time you look at him."

"Fuck."

"He feels the same way. I've seen the way he looks at you when he thinks no one is watching." She probably considered all this covert watching good practice for a career in Mil-Int. "I don't think he's figured out what it all means, but you men never know what to do with your feelings. That's why you have us."

Marnie had been the one to approach Ryan. It had been obvious since first year he was completely and irretrievably smitten, though. She said she'd only waited as long as she had because their schooling was important. Secretly, Felix thought she was more cautious than she let on, which was why this push to get him to confess his heart to his best friend of nearly ten years confused the hell out of him. Because if it went wrong, he could lose Zed. What if Zed didn't like guys? What if Felix wanting to kiss him made everything weird? Smaller things could destroy a friendship.

"Just tell him, okay? Yes, this might be the last time you're going to see him for a year or more. But love is patient, and if it's meant to be between you guys, then it will be—wherever you are, whatever you're doing. Wouldn't you be happier boarding that shuttle tomorrow knowing he's in your heart?"

No, because he'd had Zed in his heart for near on six years already and it wasn't enough.

"I'm not giving you a shirt until you promise you'll say something."

"I hate you."

"No you don't."

Hauling in a breath, Felix held it until his head spun lightly and the edges of his vision darkened. Then he let it out. "Fine, I'll say something."

"And you'll wear something other than your uniform tonight?"

"I'll wear the fancy-ass pants and shirt." He breathed in and out again, more quickly, and began unfastening his uniform pants. When Marnie didn't move, he said, "Thank you?"

She leaned into the closet to hang his plain, safe uniform shirt away. "You're welcome." The side of her face was just visible, and the fact her lips fought a smile.

"You sure Mom's not upset about me wanting to go out tonight?" Zed turned his attention from his closet to his oldest brother, Brennan, who had settled back into the cheap, student-quarters couch tucked against the wall of his dorm room. At twenty-five, Brennan looked every inch the young corporate executive, in his well-tailored suit and perfectly groomed hair. Zed grinned at Brennan's slight grimace—he could probably feel the sofa's springs digging into his butt, which was why Zed didn't sit there often—then looked back into his closet for just the right shirt.

"Did she tell you it wasn't a problem?"

"Yeah."

"Then it's not a problem," Brennan said. "*Someone's* feeling guilty."

Zed rolled his eyes and pulled out a deep blue shirt with a silvery sheen. Yeah, this would do. "I know she originally wanted to have dinner—"

Brennan chuckled. "Zed, relax. She knows this is going to be the last night with your friends for a while. Us, you'll come visit on leave, right? But everyone else…"

Everyone else would be scattered out among the stars, at training and then on their first assignments. It hit him hard at that moment that tonight was *it*. This was the last time they'd all be together at once. He'd have Emma with him, and she was awesome—a great friend who posed a great challenge, marks-wise—but her presence wouldn't quite make up for leaving his other friends behind.

Leaving Flick behind.

Don't think about that.

"Scary, huh?"

Zed looked up from the shirt clutched in his hands to see Brennan looking at him with a sort-of sad, sort-of proud expression. From somewhere, Zed summoned a weak chuckle. "Yeah."

"I can't even imagine." His low tone, the understanding in Brennan's words, they all illustrated that his oldest brother got it, even if he hadn't lived the same thing himself. "You know, there have been days I've wished you would change your mind and come work for Dad."

That was an old... well, not argument, really, but a discussion he'd had more than once with both his parents and his brother. "Bren—"

"And then you go and graduate, second in your class, standing up on stage looking just... fucking amazing in your uniform, with Mom crying and Dad just about ready to burst, he's so proud, and I realize... that's you. You were never meant to sit behind an Anatolius Industries desk and you *knew* that, ever since you were a kid." He shook his head, but it was a gesture of amazement, not denial. "You're probably more certain of your place in the galaxy than Maddox and I will ever be."

Zed swallowed hard, concentrating on conquering the lump in his throat and not breaking down, thank you very much. He didn't want to head to dinner with red, puffy eyes. "So you came here to make me embarrass myself, huh?"

Brennan snorted. "No, that's just an added bonus." Shifting on the couch, he pulled out his wallet and fiddled with the holographic interface. "There."

Zed's wallet beeped and he retrieved it from where he'd placed it on the bed as he got changed. "What'd you send—oh, damn, Brennan." He stared at the interface, his chest tight.

His brother had forwarded him a message from the administration of Shepard Academy, thanking the Anatolius family for their contribution and confirming that a permanent full scholarship would be implemented for disadvantaged kids—like Flick—who'd never see inside the doors of the school otherwise. Zed had always suspected Flick's scholarship hadn't been official—not that his father would ever admit to paying Flick's tuition. He knew how Flick would react to that news.

"Dad's real proud of him, too, you know," Brennan said quietly.

"Yeah, I know." God, his jaw ached from all these stupid emotions. "Look, you can't name it after him though, okay? He'll lose his shit."

"But—"

"Trust me. If he sees this, he's going to know that the scholarship he won was bogus, and that will just piss him off."

Brennan chuckled. "That sounds like Flick."

Zed nodded. "Tell Dad—tell him thanks."

"Tell him yourself tomorrow. We're still on for breakfast, right?" Brennan levered himself up from the uncomfortable sofa and straightened his clothes. "You need to give Mom a last opportunity to hug and kiss and be mushy."

"I know. And yes, I wouldn't miss it. Now will you go and let me get dressed?"

Brennan strode over to Zed and slung an arm around his neck, pulling him in tight. "Have fun tonight. Don't do anything I wouldn't do."

"Damn it, Bren, that means I'll be home by nine."

Brennan flicked his fingers against Zed's forehead. "Asshole."

Zed turned and grabbed his brother in a bear hug. "Love you."

Brennan made a tsking noise. "Save the mush for tomorrow."

Chapter Two

Dinner was on Zed. He didn't wave around the size of his wallet often, but for tonight, for the best friends he would probably ever have, he would. Also, he knew if he didn't, Flick would probably order the cheapest bowl of soup on the menu and the guy needed to *eat*. He'd never quite bested the habit of making do with the least amount possible.

As Zed watched Flick inhale the giant bowl of fruit he'd ordered him as a surprise dessert, a thread of worry wound through his chest. Up until now, there'd been pain at the thought of leaving Flick—an impending sense of loss. But would Flick remember to eat something more than a protein bar if Zed wasn't around to remind him? Would there be anyone to shove him toward his bunk instead of letting him stay up too late to tinker on his latest project?

Maybe Flick would find a girlfriend. Or a boyfriend. Zed frowned. That was something they'd never really talked about. Was it weird, that they never had? Usually their chats focused on the two of them, their plans, their thoughts, their in-jokes, their latest projects. He'd thought about telling Flick about his time with Dawna—losing his virginity was a big deal, right?—but it had never felt like a good thing to do. Not that Flick didn't know about it—fuck, by a day later, everyone knew Dawna had seduced him, because apparently *she* had no problems talking about it. But Zed kept the details to himself.

It would've been a good time to ask Flick about his thoughts on that. *Sex.* But… he hadn't. For some reason, he just… hadn't.

Coward.

"Zed, I can hear your brain working from over here."

Zed blinked and looked across the table at Marnie, cuddled up next to Ryan. She wore a happy, slightly dopey smile—probably thanks to the amber-colored aperitif in her hands.

"What're you thinking about, man?" Ryan prompted.

"Stuff." Zed nudged his specialty coffee with his fingers, making the handle of the cup turn. "You know."

Marnie made a disgusted noise. "We're not going to wallow. Not tonight."

Emma nodded. "She's right. Tonight is about celebrating the last six years. Celebrating us." She raised her glass. "To us."

Glasses clinked together, but Zed didn't miss the fact Flick said nothing. He was being quiet tonight—not uncharacteristically so, because Flick could brood with the best of them. Just... a lot more subdued than usual.

Zed draped an arm over Flick's shoulders and tugged him closer. "You okay?"

"Sure." With a bit of squirming, Flick retrieved his wallet and set it on the table. A couple of key selections on the holographic interface brought up a holo-recorder.

"Uh oh, Flick's collecting evidence."

"Shut up, Ryan," Flick grumbled, though Zed could hear the slight smile in his voice. "I just... keep talking, all right? I want to be able to remember your voices and... shit."

Emma practically melted—so not her, but Zed blamed the booze that had been flowing through dinner. "That's so sweet, Felix."

"Yeah, yeah."

"He's your bestie, Zed," Marnie said. "Did you know he had a secret sweetness streak?"

Zed hugged Flick a little closer. God, he was going to miss this. "I suspected."

"You did not." Flick elbowed him in the ribs, not hard. "Asshole."

"Aw, but you love me." Zed tugged at Flick again when he stiffened against him and slouched in the booth, grinning at his friends. "Okay, let's tell some tales for Flick's holo. Remember the time Marnie promised us we weren't going to get caught putting itching powder in Neal the Asshole's underwear?"

Marnie shook her head. "Hey, that wasn't my fault!"

Zed sipped at his coffee as the table degenerated into shared memories and laughter as they relived the best moments of their time at Shepard Academy. Flick was warm, solid, secure at his side, and... damn, he was going to *miss* this.

"Come dance with us!" Marnie tugged on Felix's hand, pulling him toward the cacophony of light and sound pulsing through the middle of the club.

Shaking his hand loose, Felix waved her off. "Maybe in a bit. When I find my feet."

Judging by the shape of Marnie's lips, she'd scoffed. It was hard to hear anything in the din. "You've got five minutes!" Turning, she disappeared into the throng with Ryan.

Holographic images swirled across the dancefloor, weaving streamers and ethereal forms between the writhing bodies of the dancers. Even without four shots of whatever he'd been drinking burning a path from his sinuses to his gut, Felix would have had difficulty telling fantasy from reality. The squawk and grind of the music buzzing between his temples didn't help. He continued to stare into the crowd, though, hoping for a glimpse of Zed.

There he was. Despite his height and bulk, Zed moved like quicksilver. Felix loved to watch him dance. It was as if the music moved inside Zed. Or something like that. Emma danced with him and she put on a good show too, alternately flirting with Zed and the guy behind her, hips rocking forward and back to keep both guys involved. She had one arm curled around Zed's shoulders and the other flung behind her to tease the other guy's hair.

Felix's gut clenched every time she rocked into Zed.

The holo show brightened, blotting out the dancers as the music changed tempo. Hazy starscapes pulsed through the air, spinning and contracting. Felix thought he might throw up. He looked down to find his feet, unsure if they were still attached to his body. Then he was yanked sideways. Someone had caught his wrist. He stumbled into a crush of bodies, hands flailing about for purchase. When he looked up, Emma's face loomed close to his. Too close. He could smell her breath. The weights at his shoulders were her arms.

Felix turned his head, looking for Zed, and Emma caught his cheek, unsubtly forcing him to face forward again. "He went to find the head."

"Oh." Belatedly, Felix thought to play dumb, pretend he hadn't been looking for Zed, and that she shouldn't something... something. But his thoughts were too swirly and Emma wore a grin she'd borrowed from Marnie. The "knowing grin."

Her hips bumped into his. "C'mon, loosen up. Or I'll pour another shot down your throat."

His feet had been moving, sorta. But the music hadn't caught him yet. Felix didn't dance much. Not outside of his head. Closing his eyes, he tried to feel the beat like Zed did.

Emma let go of his shoulders and grabbed his hips. "Like this. Jesus, Flick. For an athletic guy, you move like shit."

"I don't really wanna dance."

"Yeah, you do."

There was no point in arguing. Emma always got the last word. And, really, she was only looking out for him in her own way. He let Emma move his hips and gave in to the weird rhythms pulsing through the air. The holograms seemed to caress the exposed skin at the back of his neck, and the floor moved beneath his feet. Or maybe his feet were moving. Maybe he was actually dancing, and feeling freer for it. He tipped his head back and closed his eyes again. Did it matter what he looked like? No one could really see him.

Emma's hands left his hips. Felix opened his eyes to find Zed had returned. The chaotic patterns of light turned Zed's eyes to steel rather than blue, and his mouth was slanted into a sleepy-drunk smile. Felix's gut clenched tighter, as did points farther south. If Emma bumped her hips to his anytime soon, she was in for a surprise. She had turned to dance with Zed, but did the swept back arm thing to keep Felix involved, then she melted or something. Must have been the holos or the liquor swirling through his veins, because suddenly Felix was dancing with Zed.

No hands on hips or curled about shoulders, no grinding, flexing, simulated sex. Emma had taken that with her— apparently supposing they'd forget she'd gone and bump into one another by mistake. Maybe she *had* known about Felix's erection.

She'd also taken all the breathable air with her, because none existed between him and Zed. Just this weird state of expectation and temptation. A longing that didn't feel all his own. Why was Zed looking at him like that? What did the question in his eyes mean?

Maybe Felix was just doing it wrong, the dancing thing. He had grace in the gym, but not here.

Zed raised a hand as if to touch him. Felix batted it away. Instinct had him following up, pushing his palm to Zed's opposite shoulder as he sought to unbalance his opponent. Realizing what he'd done, Felix rocked back. Shit. That wasn't...

He needed air, space.

Thrusting his way through the dancers, Felix stumbled across the dark floor of the club looking for the exit. He bounced around for a while until he found the staircase leading to the roof.

What the hell?

The music and the dancers flowed around Zed, unnoticed, as he stared at Flick's fleeing back. His blood buzzed with energy even as his mind felt a bit blurry with the shots Marnie had bought all of them. He'd lost himself in the energy of the dance, appreciating Emma's moves—damn, she could roll her hips like no one's business—and then Flick had been there and he'd wanted to be closer. He'd wanted to hold him. He—

Fuck, he had a hard-on.

It wasn't the first time he'd gotten horny on the dance floor. Bodies moving, butts and groins rubbing... erections were kind of a given. But he hadn't gotten hard watching Emma.

He'd gotten hard watching *Flick*.

"Are you gonna go after him?" Marnie shouted in his ear.

He turned to her. "What?"

"Are you gonna go after him?" She arched a brow.

"I—" He stared at the crowd again.

Marnie laid a hand on his shoulder. "You're gonna regret it if you don't."

Yeah. Yeah, he would.

He ignored the part of himself that begged him to stand still and *think*. Thinking could be overrated—it was something his instructors had cautioned him about. Considering every angle was all well and good, but sometimes action had to happen on instinct. He pushed forward, through the crowd, aiming for the area where he'd lost sight of Flick. Breaking through the edge, he stumbled and caught himself against the wall. The bass beat of the music thrummed through him and he felt unsteady, as though he was walking on the deck of a ship and not a concrete floor. Was it the music making him feel that way? Or the emotions, hardly acknowledged, cascading through his mind and heart?

Stop fucking thinking.

He yanked open a nearby door to find a staircase leading up. Unless Flick had slipped back into the crowd, this is where he would have had to go—there were no other exits. Zed leaped up the stairs two by two until he reached the top of them and another door. Then he paused, filled with a certainty that opening it would lead him somewhere unknown. Somewhere he'd never considered going.

He could turn around. He could walk back downstairs and find Emma in the crowd. He felt nothing for her but friendship, but she was a good friend. An awesome friend.

Not as good as Flick, though. No one was like Flick.

He pulled the door open and stepped through.

Chapter Three

The roof was not designed for visitors. A bulky HVAC unit sprawled over one half, blocking Felix's view of the sprawling metropolis of Titusville. The other half was blessedly dark.

Felix looked up. The stars always seemed weird when viewed through an atmosphere. Closer in some inexplicable way, as though they were stitched to a blanket draped around the planet. Yet also farther away. Unattainable. Felix gulped at the humid Florida air, filling his lungs. The taste of the dancefloor lingered on his tongue, and when he licked his lips, they felt numb. The sonorous bass continued to pulse through his feet, though that might simply be a memory. The roof of the club was otherwise quiet.

A breeze whispered past his cheek. Despite having spent six years planetside, stray air currents still incited a sense of unease. Station-born always knew where the vents were. Just as they always knew the location of every accessible bulkhead and maintenance panel. Their lives could depend on such things. Air that moved under the influence of atmospheric pressure, outside of a domed habitat, was just… strange.

A pang of homesickness wound through him. Though distance could be relative, tomorrow he'd put another system between himself and Pontus Station—he'd be another step removed from his home and family—and right here, right now, it was hard to remember why he was going. Surely the AEF didn't really need another engineer.

Felix scanned the rooftop again, looking for somewhere to camp out for a while. He'd have to go back downstairs soon, or risk the party joining him. But five minutes to get settled would go a long way toward getting him through the rest of the night.

The roof access door creaked open. Someone tripped through, kicking aside the brick Felix had used to prop it ajar.

Shit.

The door swung closed with a heavy clang.

Double shit.

"I hope you told someone where you were going, because that brick you just tripped over was holding the door open."

"Flick?"

Triple shit. The very person he needed space from. "What are you doing up here?"

"I could ask you the same thing."

Nope, not playing word games with Mr. Tricky Dicky Smarty Pants. "I just needed to cool off. It was hot down there."

"Yeah." Zed moved away from the shadow of the door, and the ambient city light caught his frame, highlighting his broad shoulders, the shine of his dark hair—and the fact he had one hand wrapped around the back of his neck. It was a nervous gesture, one of his tells. "Everything okay with you? You've been kinda weird tonight."

"'M fine. Just gonna miss everyone, you know?"

"You've got the passcode to my jazer account, right?"

Felix swallowed. Jazer comms were expensive, which was why Zed wanted him to use his account rather than rely on the slower, less costly relay point or ripcomms. Neither would be the same as this, though, standing so close he could smell Zed's cologne. Talking face to face.

As always, Zed read his thoughts. "I know it's not the same, but it's not as if this is it. We're just gearing up for the next adventure."

That last brought a smile to Felix's lips. "You sounded like me just then."

Zed shrugged. "Bound to happen." He glanced over shoulder. "So what's this about the door?"

"It locks from the inside. If no one saw you come up here, then we'll have to message someone to come rescue us."

"Marnie knows we're up here." Of course she did. Zed dipped his chin and a shadow obscured his face. "Flick... is..." He gripped the back of his neck again. "Wanna sit and talk awhile? Just you and me?"

Felix argued with himself for long enough that Zed looked up again, showing his confused expression. And something else. Hurt? Not stepping toward him, not flinging himself into the wide expanse of Zed's chest, took every ounce of self-control Felix had. He'd gotten away with that when they were boys, but now? It would take more than self-control to govern what happened next.

Instead, clearing his throat, he spoke roughly. "Sure. Um, yeah."

Over near the edge of the roof, a large, square duct folded away from the bulk of the HVAC, forming a long, low bench. Felix climbed over it so they could sit facing out, with a view of the city and the stars. Zed sat next to him, close but not too close. Felix shuffled over, reducing the gap. This could be the last time he sat next to Zed like this. Probably ever. If Zed and Emma didn't hook up during specialist training, then Zed would meet someone else out there in the big, wide galaxy. This night could be the end of...

Would it be dramatic to say *all things*?

He didn't know what to say, had never known what to say, but Felix knew if he didn't say something, now, Marnie's disappointment would be the least of it. *Just do it.* He could treat it like a project, right? Start small, with a test, and then alter the plan to suit his result.

He grabbed a quick breath. "This is what I'm going to miss the most." Rocking sideways, he bumped his shoulder to Zed's. "Just you and me."

The warmth that spread through Zed's body at the innocent touch of his friend's shoulder was new. Or maybe that was just his system shaking off the effects of the dancefloor. Or, hell, maybe Flick's body acted as a windbreak.

Maybe Zed was going a little crazy. His heart was definitely beating too fast and his throat had tightened. Blood rushed through his ears, a low rumble that drowned out everything but Flick's voice. He could chalk it all up to being upset about leaving Flick tomorrow—because he was—but that explanation didn't quite hit all levels of truth. So what was it? Why was he feeling so unsettled? He didn't want to say goodbye, but the dread in his chest felt... bigger than it should.

Flick leaned away, putting space between their shoulders. Fuck, Zed had fallen into thinking-mode, letting the silence stretch too long. Making a concerted effort to shut off his brain, Zed slung an arm around Flick's shoulders and pulled the smaller man to his side.

"I'm gonna miss it too," he assured Flick. *A whole hell of a lot.*

Flick leaned into Zed's side. "Yeah?"

"Yeah." Zed squeezed Flick's shoulders and bent to press a kiss to his floppy blond curls.

He realized what he'd done just as his lips made contact with Flick's scalp. His heart thumped painfully. Physical signs of affection had always been a hallmark of their relationship, partially because Flick could be so standoffish. Being one of the few people allowed to touch him freely was a gift that Zed recognized and cherished. He never shied away from slinging an arm around Flick's shoulders or giving him a hug or ruffling his hair or... hell, he'd even given Flick's hand a squeeze once or twice when they'd both needed reassurance about something.

And then... there'd been that time with the kisses.

He didn't know if Flick remembered it. It had been shortly after they'd arrived at Shepard Academy, two weeks maybe. One day, Flick just hadn't been around—which was odd, to say the least. In those first few days, he'd clung to Zed's presence, adjusting to both the schoolwork of the Academy and being planetside for the first time. For him to disappear suddenly made no sense, but Zed had thought at first that maybe Flick just needed some space. By the second missed class, though, he'd known something was wrong. He'd started searching for Flick, and when he couldn't find any trace of him, managed to get the school administrators involved. It had still taken the rest of the day to find Flick—he'd been stuffed in a locked footlocker in an unused dorm room by one of the class assholes as a lesson, or maybe a joke.

Zed would never forget how his heart had leaped into his throat when they'd popped the lid on the footlocker. Flick had been drenched in sweat, barely conscious, limp and out of it. He'd stirred slightly as the cool air brushed his sodden curls—and then Zed had kissed him, on his forehead, his cheeks, his temples, trying to show Flick just how much he meant to him, how sorry he was that he hadn't found him sooner. In that moment, Zed had understood just how much he loved his friend.

Then a nurse had pried Flick from Zed's fingers. Eventually Zed had calmed down and when Flick didn't mention the kisses, he assumed he didn't remember them. Just as well. It would have made their friendship weird, right?

Except now he was kissing Flick again... and it wasn't weird. At all.

He lifted his lips away from Flick's head. Gently, he nudged Flick's chin around so he looked up at Zed. Zed examined the face he knew almost better than his own—and why was that? Why had he invested so much of himself into this boy—man— sitting beside him? He'd never had a friend like Flick, one who made it easier to breathe when he was around because Zed knew, beyond a shadow of a doubt, that no matter what happened, Felix Ingesson would have his back. Always. A friend who calmed him and excited him, one who made Zed want to be more. Better.

A friend he loved, with every fiber of who he was.

"Zed...?" Flick whispered.

Confusion dwelled in the breathy tone, confusion Zed couldn't dispel because he felt it too. The boner he'd had on the dancefloor returned, more insistent. But... he wasn't... he'd never felt this sort of attraction for another guy. Not that there was anything wrong with guys who wanted other guys—who cared, as long as everyone was happy? He'd just never considered...

Hadn't you? Are you sure, Zander?

Flick's hazel eyes were so fucking perfect, and his lips, parted slightly, were so fucking inviting…

Stop thinking and do.

Zed lowered his lips to Flick's. And his brain went silent.

Zed was kissing him.

Actually, Zed's lips were touching his in something like a kiss. A soft press, breath held for long enough for their lips to adhere. Felix thought about pushing him away, just briefly. His right hand clenched, fingers curling into his palm. Instead, he leaned forward, his outward breath a release of a sort.

He kissed Zed.

Their lips moved at cross purposes before catching together in the sweetest harmony. Zed's mouth softened beneath his, then firmed as he kissed back, sealing the gesture. Felix tucked his hand—fingers uncurled now—between them. He paused there, unsure if he wanted to grab Zed's shirt or push him away. Zed's lips were at his again, a firmer press this time. Felix hummed into the connection, the sound one of pleasure and confusion.

He was kissing Zed. His first kiss, and he felt as if he'd been given something divine. The tingle at his lips might as well be magic—something he had wanted so badly, he must have imagined it. Surely he wasn't imagining it.

Felix pulled back, panting softly, thoughts reeling. "Did you just… kiss me?"

Zed looked about as stunned as he felt. "I did."

"Did you, um…" Felix tugged at the curls on top of his head. "Did you mean to? Like, you didn't just sort of slip down from my head to my mouth or something?"

"No."

Zed's mouth found his once more, and this time Felix was ready for the kiss. No more prepared, but ready. He leaned in, lips parting in invitation. How he knew to do that, he had no idea. The desire to have Zed in his mouth felt as natural as the need to taste Zed's lips. To feel the brush of his tongue, to know him in this way. When the tip of Zed's tongue flicked across his lips, Felix met the play. Then it seemed their mouths were fused, and that if they were pulled apart, they'd suffocate.

Who knew kissing was so good?

Felix grabbed at Zed's shirt, the silken SFT fabric slipping beneath his fingers until he found purchase. The heat of Zed's skin radiated through, and the urge to strip the shirt away all but consumed him. The raw nature of his need shocked him. The deep thrum of it, the passionate stirring of his blood and... fuck, he was so hard.

"Wait." His lips still touched Zed's. He could taste Zed's breath. "Wait." Letting go of Zed's shirt, Felix leaned back a little more, knowing he couldn't talk with Zed's mouth so close to his. "I... Is this...? How did you know?"

"I didn't. Hell, I don't even know why I kissed you." A crease appeared between Zed's brows. "Well, yeah, I do. I think maybe I should have kissed you way before now."

Felix's heart lurched in his chest. "Or I could have done it. I... did you know I wanted to?"

Zed shook his head. The corners of his mouth had turned down and he looked sad. "Is that why you've been avoiding me today?"

"I haven't been—" A dark brow arched over a stern, steel-blue eye, and Felix swallowed the lie. "I haven't been avoiding you *all* day. Just when..." He ducked his head. "Just when we were alone. Because I had something to tell you, and I knew it was going to change everything. Or maybe not." One should hitched up in a shrug.

Zed reached for one of his hands, enfolding it in a firm, but gentle grip. His thumb caressed Felix's palm. "You can always talk to me, you know that."

"But what if I need to talk *about* you? Do you really want to hear how much I'm going to miss you? That I don't know if I can be by myself after this. How many times I've imagined kissing you. How I feel in here." He thumped his chest. "And it's too late, Zed. I was afraid, and now I've left it too late. This kiss is all we're ever going to have."

Flick's dramatic proclamation rang with truth. Zed wanted to deny it, wanted to point out that the two years they'd spend in specialist training wasn't forever—but that wouldn't be fair to either of them, would it? Fuck, why hadn't they talked about this days ago, when Flick had first started getting all quiet and un-Flick-like? Zed had known the impending separation was bothering him—he'd have to have been stupid not to see it—but he kind of thought excitement would eventually overwhelm the fear. Except he hadn't known exactly why Flick had been scared, and now that he did...

"It doesn't have to be," Zed murmured. "All that we ever have, I mean."

Something like a whimper escaped Flick's throat. "Don't. Just—don't just say that."

"I'm not." Zed nudged Flick's chin to face him again. "Hey, Felix. When have I ever lied to you?"

Flick grunted and shook his head.

"Right, never. And I'm not now."

"I don't want your pity—"

"This isn't pity." Zed blew out an exasperated breath. "It's... I don't know what it is, but it's not pity. Maybe if we'd gone out dancing before, I would've figured it out, but *someone* doesn't really like the clubs." Immediately, Zed regretted his joking tone when Flick's shoulders hunched a little more. He clasped a hand around Flick's neck, rubbing. "Hey, no, I'm not... no blame, okay? I didn't know. I didn't know you wanted to kiss me and I didn't know I *wanted* you to kiss me."

Flick peeked up at him through his unruly curls. "You never thought about it?"

"No. Well... maybe." Zed's lips screwed up into something between a grimace and a smile. "In passing. I never really thought there was something there to figure out, you know? I like girls."

Flick snorted. "Yeah, Dawna made sure the whole school knew that."

"So, I figured... I don't know what I figured." That the passing thoughts he'd had about Flick's mouth were an aberration? That the times he'd caught a glance of Flick's ass or his chest and started feeling *weird* were a fluke? Sighing, he bent forward, cradling his head in his hands for a moment before looking sideways at Flick. "Do you like both?"

"No, just..." Flick swallowed. "Just guys."

They *really* should have talked about this sooner. Zed had never really delved into his own sexuality. He'd kissed women. He'd had sex with a woman and he'd really enjoyed the act, if not the next morning. He thought that made it pretty fucking clear he was into women.

But his dick wasn't hard right now because he was thinking about a woman's flowing curves. No... he was remembering how Flick smelled, how the slightest hint of stubble had rubbed against Zed's cheeks, how his lips had felt soft yet firm and not as plump as others he'd kissed.

Flick fidgeted. "Look, maybe we should just... you know, pretend this didn't happen."

"Is that what you want?"

The hesitation before the not-so-casual shrug told Zed way more than Flick's words. "Yeah. Sure."

They could walk away. Zed could forget he'd kissed a man. It would be less confusing to just stick with one gender, right? Easier. But he knew—*he knew*—if they walked away now, like this, Flick's words would come true. That one kiss would be all they would ever have. Maybe it would be a bump in their friendship, eventually laughed off. Maybe not. The idea of not seeing Flick again after specialist training... not acceptable.

"That's not what I want." Zed lifted his head to meet Flick's gaze. Flick's eyes widened an instant before Zed cupped the back of his neck again and pulled him in for a kiss that was less tentative than their first two. Zed shuddered as their lips connected again, as though they completed a circuit. Gently, but with intent, he pushed Flick onto his back and leaned over him. The feel of Flick's legs opening to cradle Zed between them was almost enough to blow his mind.

So good. So fucking *right*.

"This okay?" Zed pulled back to gaze down at Flick, noting how big and dark his hazel eyes seemed in the dim lighting. "I'm not hurting you, am I?"

Flick shook his head vehemently and Zed thought that the answer would be the same even if he had a stunner in his hand. "No, it's good. I..." Almost involuntarily, it seemed, Flick's body arched and he pressed his groin against Zed's.

Fireworks. That was the only way Zed could describe it. He closed his eyes to shut out the sight of Flick's mouth falling open, otherwise this was going to be done way too quickly. "G-God. You ever done this before?"

Flick rubbed against him again. "No, but—"

Zed's eyes snapped open. "Never? Kissing?"

Flick's gaze slid sideways.

Shit. *Shit.* Zed lowered himself, snaking his arms under Flick to hold him in a full-body, way-more-than-friends hug. "I don't really know what the fuck I'm doing here, but... do you want this?"

"Yes." Flick's voice was shaky with need.

Zed did too. The responsibility of being Flick's first time humbled him, but now that it was here, a possibility, he was all-in. He wanted to make this good. He wanted Flick to know he was loved. But taking this step scared him, too. He remembered what he'd been like the morning after he'd slept with Dawna, all but convinced it meant they were supposed to be together. Here, now, he'd give his left nut to have the time with Flick to explore this for more than just one night—but asking Flick to wait or making promises based on just these few hours, or expecting to base something long-distance on feelings so newly uncovered...

It wouldn't be fair to either of them.

He drew in a shuddering breath. "Then here's the deal. Tonight, I'm yours. I want to share this with you. I want to be your first." Zed swallowed, feeling like acid was stripping the lining of his esophagus. "But not your only, Flick. Promise me."

Chapter Four

Felix pushed Zed off him, which he wouldn't have been able to do if Zed hadn't been ready to go. Zed had always been bigger than him. Broader across the shoulders, taller. Just... more. Felix felt the loss immediately, as if he'd stepped out into a vacuum. Beneath his stupid fancy shirt and pants, his skin itched and tingled. His cock ached. He was so hard. Zed was too, and the memory of their erections bumping together made him want to moan.

Felix rolled off the wide duct and stood. He couldn't catch his breath. He couldn't think. But Zed's words rolled around and around in his head. Like the stars overhead, they wheeled when they should be fixed points. *Not your only.*

It was stupid to feel the way he did. Zed was right *here.* They'd kissed. They could do more. But Zed didn't want him in the same way.

"Flick?" Zed formed a bulky shadow next to him.

Felix could smell his skin, his sweat. Taste him on his lips and tongue. "This isn't what I want," he said, cringing at the lie. He craved Zed with obsessive need.

Dipping his chin, Zed gave a short nod and it seemed that would be that. Tension continued to snap between them, but Felix knew if he moved forward, by even a step, the presence of Zed would capture him and he'd never pull free.

And Zed didn't want that.

"This is Marnie's fault," Felix muttered, pulling out his wallet.

Pacing toward the door, he tried pinging Marnie and got no answer. He couldn't say he was surprised. But when he got to the door, he almost laughed. No padlock, but as the door opened outward, there was no handle on this side, and no panel. Nothing for him to hack, nothing for him to bash into submission. Nothing but him and Zed and the stars.

God, he hated feeling trapped like this.

Raising a fist, Felix pounded on the smooth metal. "Marnie? I know you're there. Open the fucking door." He tucked his wallet back into his pocket and attacked the door with two hands. "Marnie! This isn't going to work. You're just pissing me off."

A warm hand closed around his shoulder. Felix shrugged it off. Zed grabbed him again and Felix turned toward him, right fist cocked and ready.

Zed ducked sideways. "Jesus."

"Just keep your hands off me."

Straightening, Zed held up both hands as he took a step back. "Talk to me. Tell me what's going on. 'Cause one minute you're grinding against me, the next you're taking a swing at me."

"I told you I didn't want it. Can't we leave it at that?"

"No. Because you're lying to me. Since when did you start lying to me, man?"

Chest tightening, Felix looked up at the stars and wished he could just launch himself into the sky. Take off, disappear, or maybe cease to exist. He didn't hear Zed step forward, but he felt him, and took a step back.

"Flick, please. Let's not end things like this. You're my best friend. Always."

Felix met Zed's questioning gaze. "What if I want to be more? Always."

Zed shook his head. "Why would you want that? You've got your whole life ahead of you. Training, and then you're going to travel the galaxy. With your skills, you'll see the whole fleet. I can't be the one to hold you back."

"You've never held me back. It's because of you I've got this far. And I don't know if I can..." Felix swallowed. "You're going to have Emma and Marnie and Ryan are going to Mil-Int together and I'm going to be alone. By myself." He took another step back. "I told Marnie this was a bad idea. You didn't need to know any of this."

"I already knew most of it."

Felix shook his head. "You don't know all of it."

"Then tell me."

He didn't want to, but what did it matter? There would be no perfect time for his confession, and they were out of time to fix what he'd probably just broken. So why not throw the words out there? Maybe then Zed would feel it. Maybe he'd hurt. Or, just maybe, he'd pick them up and... carry them. Hold the words close until they could see each other again.

Drawing on every mote of courage in his lean frame, Felix squared his shoulders and looked Zed square in the eye. "I love you."

Zed almost, *almost* replied with a casual "I love you, too," because he did. He didn't know exactly when he'd started loving Flick—sometime shortly after they'd met, probably—and he knew it wasn't quite like what he felt for his two older brothers. But one look in Flick's eyes told Zed that he was dead serious about this love thing. This wasn't some declaration of brotherly fealty, but the real deal, the heart fully invested, the can't-breathe-without-you sort of love.

And he was telling Zed this *now*?

"Why the fuck didn't you tell me sooner?" Zed turned and kicked at nothing, needing to take out his frustration. Glancing over his shoulder, he saw Flick deflate, as though Zed's words had punctured something important. "Goddamn it, we talk about everything."

"Not that," Flick said, his voice small.

Zed blew out a breath, then agreed, "No, not that." But they should have. He speared his fingers through his coiffed hair, which had already mostly been wrecked by the dancing, and tugged. It was a Flick gesture, one he'd picked up years ago. He tilted his head to look up at the stars, winking through the atmosphere as if they knew the answer to this problem but weren't going to tell anyone.

Flick loved him. Like that.

Fuck.

"I love you too, you know?" Zed sighed. "But I don't know if… if it's the same as what you feel. I mean, I feel better when you're with me. I love spending time with you and sharing jokes and stories, watching a holo, whatever. But I *just* figured out that maybe guys turn me on just as much as girls." And that was a revelation he would need to examine in way more detail, but not now. "So I don't know. If we had more time…"

A soft, sad chuckle left Flick's lips. "Yeah, if we had more time."

Zed closed the distance between the two of them and carefully reached out to rest his hands on Flick's shoulders, prepared to field another punch. The fight seemed to have abandoned his friend, though, leaving him smaller than moments ago.

"What I meant before?" he said softly. "I don't want you to not live your life because you're waiting for something that might not happen. Okay? We're probably not going to be able to do more than exchange the occasional jazer—"

"That would be enough!"

Zed rubbed Flick's shoulders. "No, it wouldn't. And I know you, Felix Ingesson. You'd use those messages as an excuse to cordon yourself off and not even consider the possibilities around you."

"But—"

Whatever Flick was about to say was cut off by an explosion overhead. Zed whipped around to watch brightly colored sparkles cascade through the night sky, falling to earth like a hundred tiny meteorites. Crackles chased another boom, then another, and a holo played across the darkness.

"Congratulations to the Shepard Academy Class of 2256," Zed read, his voice quiet. He looked back at Flick, taking in the sight of his best friend's features illuminated by red, then blue, then green, then red again.

Beautiful.

A sudden urge to trace the lines of Flick's face with his fingertips threatened to overwhelm him, but Zed tamped it down.

Why had he never really noticed how strong Flick's face was before? In the years since they'd met, Flick had filled out—age and good food conspiring to strip the slim boyishness from his features. He'd never be the sort of guy that you'd expect to find on the front lines—not like Zed, who was built like a truck and only seemed to get wider with every passing year—but that was okay. Flick was a fix-it guy, someone who dwelled behind the scenes. His delicate fingers were magic.

"C'mon. Sit with me." Zed pulled at one of Flick's shoulders, then released his grip. "We don't have to talk anymore, if you don't want to." Truthfully, it didn't matter if they spent the rest of the night in silence. Zed just wanted to be here, with Flick, whatever the night brought, because damned if he knew when they'd have a chance to do this again. If they ever did. "Might as well enjoy the show, right?"

Flick glanced at the sealed door, then nodded, his body language transmitting his reluctance with every movement. Zed held back a sigh. Maybe he should just kiss Flick again—stir the flames of horniness so high they forgot everything else. It was tempting, so bloody tempting, but Flick had made it pretty clear he wanted everything or nothing at all.

Zed wished he could give him everything. If they only had more time…

He sat heavily on the duct and leaned back on his hands to watch the lightshow overhead. Flick settled beside him, close enough that Zed could just barely feel the heat radiating from him, but not touching.

"Pretty," Flick said after a few more booms.

Zed nodded as the names of the graduates began streaming by. His was third, after Neal Aarons and Kiro Amago. He didn't say anything as the names progressed through the alphabet, but when Flick's appeared, he bumped his friend's shoulder. Just a reminder that he was there, they'd made it and whatever came next, they'd be all right.

God, he hoped they would be.

Chapter Five

His name in lights. The flare of familiar letters brought a lump to Felix's throat. He wished his father could see it. Quickly, before the holo faded, he pulled out his wallet and snapped a few pictures. He missed reading the next few names while he chose the best one to share with his family.

Zed leaned over his shoulder—as he'd done so many times before—to watch him tap out the ripcomm. "They'll be so proud of you."

Felix nodded, his throat a little too tight for words. He sent off the message and tucked his wallet away. He looked back up at Zed, who remained inclined toward him, as if still reading over his shoulder. If not for this... man, they were men, now. If not for Zed, he wouldn't sitting here with his heart swollen with such a mixture of emotion. Pride, anxiety, a little fear, and a big and achy thing called love. But he wouldn't exchange a minute of it— not for all the credits in the galaxy. Because his family was proud of his accomplishments, and his career with the AEF would almost guarantee he could take care of them. Because he'd had the opportunity to learn from the best, and to share the experience with the best. The Fantastic Five: Zed, Emma, Marnie, Ryan and Felix.

No distance could separate them, not after the last six years of friendship. Nothing should be able to separate him and Zed—but what could drive them apart was him not acknowledging this night, what he had right here, right now. He wanted more, but he could have this. One night, one special night. What better memory than sharing all of his firsts with the man he loved?

Reaching up, he caressed Zed's cheek. It was generally accepted that Zander Anatolius was handsome, but Felix saw beneath the strong brows, straight nose, high cheekbones and sensuous mouth. He saw through those cool blue eyes to the soul beneath. He flashed back to ten years before, to a younger and more rounded version of this face. Zed stuck in the ductwork of Pontus Station after having given chase when Felix stole his wallet. He remembered how the expression on Zed's face had stopped him. The combination of admiration and challenge—and the sure knowledge that if Felix helped him out of the duct, he'd be grateful rather than angry. Zed was a good person. The perfect friend and the best sort of ally. Even at eight years old, Felix had known that Zed could show him the galaxy.

Zed leaned into his caress, eyelids fluttering down. Felix traced his thumb along one dark eyebrow, smoothing the short, bristly hairs. It only seemed right he should tend the other, then drop a kiss to each closed eye. The scent of Zed's skin slipped inside him—the same as always, but now different, too. Because now he knew what Zed's lips tasted like, and how they felt against his.

Felix kissed the tip of Zed's nose. A puff of air tickled his chin as Zed chuckled softly. Sensing an eye might open, Felix pressed his thumb gently to the lid. "No."

Zed made a small noise in his throat, but complied, leaving his eyes closed. Felix continued worshiping his face, dropping a kiss to the hint of a dimple in his left cheek, then his right. He kissed the corner of Zed's mouth and tickled the seam of his lips with his tongue. Zed groaned softly, lips parting. Felix kissed the bottom, sucking gently on the plump flesh before releasing it to kiss him squarely on the mouth.

There, his seduction technique faltered. The kiss was awkward, more friendly than sexy. A niggle of anxiety poked Felix in the chest. Before he could listen to it, respond to it, Zed tilted his head and their mouths slid together. Then they were kissing. Properly.

Zed captured the sides of his face with his large hands. In their embrace, Felix felt safe and protected. He had to drag his thoughts away from there, though, lest he spiral back into fearing everything he'd miss after tonight. Instead, he willed his mind to blank, and when that didn't work, he focused on the sounds Zed made while they kissed. The soft breaths, the hum deep in his throat. The swish of fabric as they moved together. The suck and pull of their lips.

Zed's tongue teased his and Felix reveled in the sensual caress. Who would have thought having someone else's tongue in his mouth would feel so good, and so fucking necessary? Needing a deeper breath, Felix pulled his lips from Zed's and nuzzled the side of his face. The rasp of stubble against his cheek sent a thrill across his skin. His nipples tingled. His dick fought the confines of his fancy pants. Again.

Overhead, the sound of fireworks faded away. The sky might still be lit by holos, but Felix no longer cared. He was making his own memories—and he wasn't going to think about what he'd do with them until later. Tomorrow. Next week.

Zed leaned into him, obviously intending to lay him back again. Putting both hands to Zed's chest, Felix reversed his direction, encouraging Zed to lie back instead. Zed complied with a sweet willingness that spoke louder than words. But he did grasp Felix's elbows, pulling him along for the ride, and as soon as Felix was settled against his chest, Zed's hands slipped up under his the back of his shirt.

"Oh!" The warmth of Zed's palms against his skin was electric. Felix arched into him, gasping as their erections bumped together. Surely they'd just been struck by lightning. "Fuck, does it always feel like this?" Zed would know, right? Zed had experiences he didn't.

"No." Zed's hips pushed upward. "This is for you."

It almost hurt, which shouldn't make sense, but Felix had jacked off enough times to appreciate the sensitivity of his equipment in certain situations. Apparently it wasn't all due to over handling.

Shifting slightly so that he knelt between Zed's legs, Felix tugged Zed's shirt free of his pants. Immediately, he smoothed his hands upward, but he couldn't get to where he wanted. Pulling his hands back out, he reached for the buttons, hesitating at the first. "I want to see you, is that okay?"

Zed met his question with a dark and hooded gaze. "Yes."

It wasn't as if he'd never seen Zed without his shirt before, but now it was different. Now he saw the cut of Zed's muscles, and the way his torso tapered from broad shoulders to lean hips, through a haze of lust. He wanted to bite one of those small, flat nipples. He wanted to trace his tongue down the groove between Zed's abs.

Zed shrugged the shirt from his shoulders and reached for Felix's buttons. A blush stung Felix's cheeks and he knew that once Zed undid his shirt, the flush of color would be visible across his chest. Would Zed think he was too...lean?

Once both their shirts were on the ground, Felix attacked Zed's chest with small kisses and bites, starting with the sweep of his collarbones and working his way down. Zed arched beneath him. His nipples were like tiny pebbles, his abs smooth and firm. The fine hair between his pecs tickled Felix's lips. Would he grow more? Felix hoped so. The hair was sexy.

When he got down to Zed's navel, he could smell the musk of his crotch. Felix palmed the bulge beneath Zed's waistband and squeezed, drawing the best sound yet from deep down in Zed's chest. A groan vibrated between them. Felix's nuts tightened and his dick pulsed.

Before he could attack Zed's belt, hands caught his and pulled him upward. Felix settled into Zed's chest, sighing as their skin brushed together and stuck in places, from the humidity of the night and their sweat. Zed felt so good against him. Under him.

"My turn to explore," Zed rumbled, before claiming his mouth in another kiss.

At eighteen years of age, Zed had a few sexual experiences under his belt. There was the encounter with Dawna and its widely broadcast success, yeah, but there had been other kisses with classmates, too, and girls' hands rubbing him through his pants. There'd even been one when he was fifteen who was brave enough to reach underneath his waistband and stroke him skin-on-skin for the whole minute it took him to come.

But this… nothing compared to this.

He rolled over, positioning his hand at the back of Flick's head to make sure those bouncy blond curls didn't make the wrong kind of contact with the hard surface of the wide duct. Slowly, gently, he lowered Flick's head and looked down at him, surprised at the kick his heart gave as the meager light teased highlights from Flick's hair.

"I don't know what I'm doing," he admitted, his voice shaky with need. How could he when it was only hitting him now how fucking beautiful Flick was? Why hadn't he realized it sooner?

"Me neither." Flick's smile wasn't wide, but it was genuine. Certain. Whatever switch had gotten tripped to get them back to this point, it wasn't getting flipped off again. "Just do what feels good."

Do what feels good. Yeah, okay, he could try.

A breeze kissed his skin, drawing up goosebumps across his neck. He ignored it, his attention solely on the man lying beneath him. For a moment, he just stared at Flick's pecs, noting how his nipples were already pebbled and begging for a touch.

Would they be as sensitive as a woman's?

Bending down, he captured one in his mouth. Flick arched beneath him, letting out a choked cry, and Zed hummed in appreciation of his discovery. He rolled the tight bud between his teeth, then sucked on it, loving the curses falling from Flick's lips. The lean body beneath him bucked and writhed—and *fuck*, that was such a turn on. When he drew back, exposing the reddened, wet nipple to the night air, Flick whimpered.

"Jesus, Joseph and Mary, I almost came," he panted.

Zed grinned, absurdly pleased with himself. "Yeah?"

"I never knew… God, I never knew…" A flick of Zed's tongue to the other nipple was answered with a deep groan. "Need… Zed, need more… oh my God…"

Zed kissed his way down Flick's torso, trying not to think. *Do what feels good.* This felt good—so damned good, with the sounds Flick was making. Zed realized that he would do just about anything to encourage those helpless noises to continue. He paused at the waistband of Flick's pants, hovering over the bulge straining at his fly, and some instinct made him inhale deeply, drawing Flick's scent into his lungs.

His arousal, humming along at a steady pace while he'd explored Flick's skin, spiked. Even after six years planetside, Flick smelled like a space station—there was a tang to his scent that reminded Zed of circuits and a contained atmosphere. Beneath that was a rich undertone—something that shouted *man!* in the lizard part of Zed's brain, the part that was all *desire* and *need* and fuckloads of *want*. If he'd had any doubts lingering about whether or not his own gender turned him on, the steady pulsing of his cock at that incredible scent would have erased them.

He flipped open the clasp at the top of Flick's zipper and pulled it down, tugging at Flick's pants and underwear as he did so. Flick lifted his butt so Zed could free his erection, which slapped against his stomach, the sound of skin against skin a perfect counterpoint to their ragged breaths.

Zed stared. He couldn't help it. It was the first time he'd seen a hard dick that wasn't his own, and he wasn't so far gone on lust that he didn't want to categorize the differences. Flick was longer than he was—but not by much—and a little thinner, with a perfectly proportioned crown currently dripping pre-come over his abdomen. His balls were tight against the base of his cock and graced with bristly hair just a shade or two darker than that on his head. Zed trailed a fingertip along the prominent vein and Flick's cock twitched.

Flick whimpered. "God, the way you're looking at me..."

Emboldened by the instinctive movement of Flick's hips, Zed wrapped his hand around his erection and jacked.

"Fuck!" Flick's cry was strangled, as though he was desperate to hold a part of himself back.

That wouldn't do. Zed wanted all of him, right here, on this rooftop alongside him. He wanted... well, something he'd never experienced himself, and not something he'd ever done to someone else—obviously—but there was a reason porn existed, right? A boy had to get his education somewhere.

Don't think, just do.

Zed pressed his tongue flat against Flick's cock and licked, all the way up from balls to tip—then engulfed the crown and sucked. Flick's whole body spasmed, as though Zed was made of electricity, and nonsensical words poured out of his mouth. Babbling... he'd made Flick babble.

And damn, he liked the feel of a hard cock on his tongue.

It wasn't something he'd daydreamed about but now that he was here, doing this, he wondered why he hadn't. The salty-bitter drops of pre-come leaking from Flick's tip tasted amazing. Flick thrust upward, out of control, and Zed gagged as the erection slammed to the back of his throat. Lesson learned. He encircled the base with one hand to better control the depth. Retching would not be sexy.

"Fuck, fuck, *fuck*," Flick moaned. "Don't stop, please don't..."

In answer, Zed sucked harder, faster. He fluttered his tongue into the slit, reveling at the concentrated flavor of Flick, and groaned. His own cock pounded against his pants, desperate for a touch, a brush, a thought, anything. But all that truly mattered in this moment was Flick. Flick's pleasure, Flick's love.

"Gah... Zed, I'm... *fuck*!" Flick's body curved upward, then released. Come flooded Zed's mouth—the taste more bitter than the pre-come. He swallowed some, gagged a little, and pulled back to coax Flick through his orgasm with a hand instead of his mouth. Spit and more covered his chin and he swiped at it with the back of his free hand. Flick shook with tremors, coming down from what looked like an amazing high—and Zed had done that, brought his friend to the pinnacle of physical pleasure.

It wouldn't get awkward now, would it?

Zed had sucked his brains out through his cock. Felix couldn't think. Hell, he could barely breathe. Coming had never felt like this before. Of course, he'd only ever had the comfort of his hand.

A mouth? Holy shit. Zed had sucked his cock. Kissed it, licked it, taken it inside his mouth and sucked it.

Why hadn't he told Zed he loved him a year ago?

Zed looked kinda dazed.

"That was 'mazing," Felix said, tongue refusing to work properly. How was he ever going to return this favor without a working tongue? Wait. Was he really thinking about doing this to Zed? Felix's thoughts stuttered again before clearing with a resounding *fuck yeah*.

Zed had moved back, and a sense of loss wound through Felix—not just because Zed had let go of his penis. Reaching down to pull up his pants, Felix tilted his head sideways to get another look at Zed's face, and caught sight of an expression that didn't visit Anatolius features very often: *hesitance*.

"Hey," Felix murmured.

Zed wouldn't meet his eyes.

Nope, they weren't going to do this now, whatever it was Zed was thinking of doing. They were not going to stop and think. Talk it out, remind each other of the fact this was a one night deal. Felix refused to believe that, anyway. When Zed stepped onto his shuttle in the morning, he'd be taking a piece of Felix with him, and leaving a piece of himself behind. What they shared could never be explored in one night. Hadn't Marnie said love was patient? Felix wasn't known for patience, but he could be a persistent bugger.

He tucked himself away and reached for Zed, hauling him back in. "Want to taste myself on you," he said, lifting his chin for a kiss.

Zed kissed him and it was... weird. The flavor of Zed's mouth altered his taste. Felix couldn't say if it was good or bad, but it was definitely sexy. He kissed Zed until the rumble started again, until Zed seemed committed to what they were doing once more. Then Felix began pushing him backward. They really should have scouted a better location than an air conditioning duct for this. But it was nearly as wide as a dorm room bed and they did have a locked door. And the beauty of the stars strung overhead probably couldn't be equaled.

Felix pulled at Zed's belt.

"You don't have to," Zed said, catching his hands.

"'S rude to talk when you're being kissed." Felix's lips moved over Zed's. "Besides, where you lead, I follow. Always been like that."

"Not always. I've followed you many a time."

"Usually into trouble." Grinning, Felix pressed another kiss to Zed's lips and discovered that smiling widely made kissing difficult. Their mouths didn't line up anymore. He grabbed at the hard ridge behind Zed's fly and squeezed. Zed's moan changed the shape of his lips, and the kissing got all serious again.

Belt undone, zip tugged down, Felix urged Zed to lift his hips. He pushed Zed's pants down to his thighs, too eager to get to the good stuff to bother getting them down any farther. He slid a hand inside Zed's underpants and grasped his length.

"God, you're so hot." He meant temperature wise, but Zed could take it any way he wanted. His cock *was* hot, and heavy against Felix's palm. He squeezed. Zed gasped and groaned. Arched upward. Felix let go long enough to tug Zed's underwear down and took a moment to appreciate what he'd unveiled. Thick, hard, and ruddy, with a slight kink to the left. Felix took a hold of the shaft and straightened it. Pre-come beaded the divot at the top, glistening in the starlight. Felix leaned forward to lick it.

Tasted… not entirely pleasant. But he liked it anyway. It was Zed, and he reckoned with practice, he could get used to it. Learn to love it. And the way Zed was groaning? Yeah…

A moment of uncertainty caught him as he prepared to wrap his lips around the crown. What if he did this wrong? What if his teeth got in the way? Would he choke? He'd heard Zed making a noise like he might have tried to swallow too much. What if he figured out this was the best thing ever, and didn't get a chance to suck Zed's cock again? Ever.

Shut up and suck it, Flick.

He opened his mouth and swallowed Zed's cock. Beneath him, Zed shuddered and moaned. His hips thrust upward and the head of his cock nudged the back of Felix's throat. Gagging,

Felix pulled back and followed Zed's example of using his hand as a depth gauge.

Don't suck past this point.

Sucking to down to his fingers was amazing, though. The taste, the feel of Zed's rigid flesh against his tongue. The way Zed's cock seemed to pulse in his mouth. And having just had Zed's mouth around his own precious had taught him a couple of things: pressure was king, and there was nothing more awesome than the feeling of being wrapped up tight—and of having something to push into and against.

"Oh God, oh God," Zed whispered-moaned.

With his other hand, Felix cupped Zed's heavy sac. Zed grunted and jerked. More bitter fluid met Felix's tongue. Rounding his lips, Felix sucked up and down in a steady rhythm—four, maybe five times?—then Zed pushed at his shoulders.

"Coming!"

Felix pulled away.

Zed's head tipped back and his hips thrust up. Felix jacked him once more and he came, jetting upward, his whole body following. Felix wished he'd stayed down there to catch it in his mouth, even though he knew he'd have coughed and spat and... well, Zed probably wouldn't have noticed. He was still thrusting and coming. And coming. Jesus, how long had it been since he'd last jerked off?

Felix lowered his lips to kiss the wet and shiny head of Zed's softening dick and Zed shuddered again. "Oh God."

Felix licked.

"Fuck!"

Felix hummed against the sticky warmth.

"Stop. You're killing me."

Pulling back, Felix licked his lips. He felt like a cat licking cream from its whiskers. Zed caught him around the back of the neck with one of those big old hands of his and pulled him down for a kiss. Felix went willingly, barely hesitating when his almost dry stomach met Zed's damp and slick skin. The kiss was a tasting sample, both of them licking and sucking at one another's tongues. Then Zed's arms banded around his back, pulling him closer, and they cuddled.

Felix dropped his head into the crook of Zed's neck and shoulder and nuzzled the sweat-dampened skin there, inhaling the scent of Zed's soap and cologne. He could feel Zed's heart beating steadily against his chest. Below his hips, Zed's limp cock smooshed somewhere near his own.

Felix never wanted to move. Ever. He wanted to stay right here, in the secure circle of Zed's arms. It had been so long since they'd lain like this. Not that they'd ever formed the habit of cuddling half naked, semen cooling between them. But they'd shared a room for two years, and even after, they'd often spent the night together, squashed side by side in the same bed, Zed making music and Felix reading comics. Conversation had been optional, because so often they hadn't needed words. Just being together had been enough.

Tears pricked Felix's eyes. He tucked an arm around the back of Zed's neck and pulled him close. "Going to miss you," he said to Zed's neck.

"Going to miss you too." Words felt more than heard as they rumbled through Zed's chest. Zed's arms tightened around him. "But I know you're going to do great. Gonna make us all proud. The fleet needs engineers like you."

"And heroes like you."

"Flick—"

"Don't say anything else." Felix pushed upward, against the circle of Zed's arms, and pressed a hard kiss to his mouth. "Let's just keep this, okay? Let this be…" What? He so desperately wanted to tell Zed he loved him again. Speak it against his lips with the taste of sex. "Let this be our night. Like you said." Zed had said one night, but whatever. "Can we… can we not talk about what's next for a while? Can we just remember what was?" Damn, his throat was closing. "I don't want to forget all the fun things we've done over the last six years."

"Last ten," Zed murmured.

"Right, like the time I talked you into stealing those strawberries from the Upper Market on Pontus."

Zed's sudden laugh quickly softened into a chuckle and his cheeks bunched up just like they always did when he found something very amusing. He moved a hand up to muss Felix's curls. "You are such a bad influence on me."

"Pfft." Felix leaned away and stood so he could fasten his pants properly. Idly, he picked at the drying mess on his stomach. Ugh. "We should probably clean up and get dressed before Marnie decides to rescue us."

No matter how they wanted to keep reality at bay, the fact was, they couldn't. It intruded, an unwelcome interloper slipping between them as they sat, sides pressed together and arms over each other's shoulders, watching the stars. Zed didn't mention what awaited them in the morning. No more talk of training or what the future held. Instead, he delved into memories, every single good memory he could think of, and tried to pretend that the pain in his chest wasn't his heart breaking.

Maybe he did love Flick *like that*—God, he didn't know, not for sure. He needed to think, to study the emotions from all angles. He didn't say anything, didn't let on about the turmoil roiling around in his chest. It wouldn't make things any easier and Flick already knew how much Zed cared for him. That counted more than three little words that may or may not be true.

Three little words that would hobble Flick.

They had fallen silent by the time the sky lightened with false dawn. Flick leaned on Zed, his breathing even, and Zed had fallen into a sort of not-quite doze. Rattling at the roof door made him jerk fully awake.

Flick snorted and sat up, blinking blearily. "Wha?"

The door opened. Zed wasn't surprised to see Marnie, Emma and Ryan spill through—really, the only surprising thing was that it had taken this long for their friends to find them.

Or—by the way Marnie was smiling at him and Flick—maybe not so surprising after all.

"Prop the door!" Flick shouted.

"I got it, I got it," Ryan said, fitting the brick back into the doorway to keep it ajar. "You guys have a nice night?"

Zed glanced at Flick and hoped the darkness and his olive skin tone helped to mask his blush. He cleared his throat. "We had a great view of the fireworks."

"There were fireworks?" Emma flopped down beside Flick.

"With our names and everything," Flick told her.

Marnie and Ryan settled on the other side of Zed. "That would have been cool to see," Marnie said, glancing at Ryan. "Really romantic."

"Uh huh." From Flick's tone—and the glare he shot in Marnie's direction—he clearly thought she still had something to do with stranding them up here. Which was ridiculous, because how could she have known Flick would come up here, or that Zed would come after him and be too stupid to make sure the door could be opened from this side before letting it close? "Figured you guys would all be fast asleep by now."

Ryan snorted. "Hell no. We've been—ow." Rubbing the ribs that Marnie had elbowed, he continued. "Looking for you."

"There were so many places you could have disappeared to." Marnie's brown, almond-shaped eyes were all innocence.

"Marn, I really hope Mil-Int teaches you to have a better poker face," Zed said. She caught his gaze, hers questioning, and he gave a little shake of his head.

He didn't know what he meant by the gesture, but Marnie seemed to understand. She was good like that, seeing beneath façades and words to get to the truth. And the truth was... he just didn't fucking know where they went from here.

No, that was kind of a lie. From here, they went to specialist training. After specialist training, they would do their first postings. And then...

And then, who knew. He couldn't see that far into the future, couldn't even imagine it. Trying to out-think it, out-plan it, wasn't going to happen. They would all just have to live it.

He squeezed Flick against his side and brushed his lips over Flick's temple. "You're not going to lose me," he whispered. It was a promise—not the one he wanted to give Flick, but the only one he could.

Flick shivered, whether from the breeze or Zed's words, he didn't know. "Ditto," he murmured.

It would have to be enough.

REUNION

It's been four years since Zander and Felix graduated from Shepard Academy. Four years since they shared a single night together. Now they have five days of shore leave to see if their friendship is still as strong as it was…and to see if the promises they didn't want to make back then might be possible now.

"Reunion" is set approximately nine years before *Chaos Station* (Chaos Station #1)

Chapter One

Hemera Station, 2260

Felix could have waited at the hostel. Done the cool thing and cornered a table in the bar downstairs, lined up some empty shot glasses and pretended to be simultaneously drinking, flirting and solving complex equations on his wallet. Or he could have left a key to his room at the desk with a note. Waited sprawled across the bed in a state of partial undress, feigning sleep. Nah, he'd have gone nuts alone in the dark or taken himself in hand, and neither would have been the picture he wanted to present when a certain someone opened the door.

Instead, he researched (hacked) the passenger manifests from several incoming transports, assigned a gate to the last one, jumping it to the head of the queue, and crossed the docking hub of Hemera Station at a leisurely stroll. No arriving harried and sweaty for him, and no hanging out in space for Zander Anatolius while the incompetent boobs piloting his shuttle stared at the pretty lights and tried to remember their training.

But the wait, short as it promised to be, might kill him.

It'd been four years since he'd last seen Zed—since he'd stood on a rooftop and declared his heart. Heat stung Felix's cheeks at the memory. He'd embarrassed himself and probably Zed...but he'd also won a single night with the man he loved. A handful of hours filled with the wordless promises he'd promised not to make. Kisses filled with the taste of Zed; his skin, his mouth, his sweat. The essence of him.

He'd also promised to forget. He never had.

Scrubbing his hands against the worn patches of smart fiber along the front of his pants, Felix paced up and down the dock lounge. He arrived at a row of molded plastic seats, each stuck to a long, metal beam. The garish pink curve of each seat looked something like an exotic flower, the whole construction some sort of alien vine. His bum caressed one of the seats for ten seconds before Felix leapt up to pace the length of the vine again. Then he strolled to the window in defiance of the old adage regarding watched things never doing whatever the fuck they were supposed to do.

To his left, Felix could just see the faint outline of the corona surrounding the distant gate. The glint of light to his right was reflected sunlight. The darkness of space blanketed everything else, but it wasn't a frightening sort of darkness. Not small or oppressive. Myriad lights circled the station, bright against the thousand thousand pinprick stars strung behind.

Heart drumming a frantic but familiar rhythm, he scanned the lights, looking for Zed's transport. "Where are you?"

It'd taken six months for him to answer Zed's frequent ripmails with something more than: *I'm fine. Very busy.* Then he'd shared the fact he'd made a friend in specialist training, a *close* friend, and let Zed draw his own conclusions. Felix hadn't wanted to say he'd moved on, but he had. Or he'd tried to, even though he tasted ash every time he thought about the fact Zed also had a *close* friend. A girlfriend. It wasn't until each of them had walked away from those relationships that their own friendship had started to come back together, via ripmail and the occasional jazer—on Zed's credit, of course. Long, rambling conversations that sometimes approached nights at the Academy when they'd lain side by side in a bunk, or up on the roof, and talked about nothing. When they'd simply spent time together.

They'd rebuilt the stack of bricks forming their friendship and these five days together on Hemera Station were to be the cement. So maybe he should stop fretting and head back to the hostel. Line up those shot glasses.

A tremor pushed through the floor beneath Felix's boots. Looking up, he saw the familiar Allied Earth Forces logo as Zed's transport nudged the docking hub and the clamps engaged. Felix scrubbed his hands over his thighs again and took a deep breath.

No amount of oxygen could calm the butterflies performing zero-g maneuvers in his stomach. Or dry the sweat at the back of his neck, down the column of his spine, at the back of his knees and, for the love of all those useless gods, on his palms.

This was it! Zed was here. Felix felt his mouth curving into a big, stupid grin. He wrestled his features back into a soldierly countenance right away, but knew that the minute Zed stepped through the 'lock, he'd be grinning like a boy again. He strolled over to the hatch and tried not to twitch in place.

If Zed ever acquired a position in which he trained recruits or new officers, he was going to be sure to tell them two things. One, be smart about your choice of lovers. Everyone screwed around, that was just a given, but only stupid men and women got caught. And two, concussions really, really sucked.

His fingers found the scar at the back of his head, a gesture he found himself making more and more frequently, and one he was trying to not turn into a habit. He redirected his fingers to his shorn hair—he'd shaved it rather than sport a bald patch among the rest. After a couple of months, it wasn't quite a buzz cut anymore, but still a lot shorter than he used to wear it at the Academy.

Would Flick like it?

Zed's fingers found his scar again and he grumbled, then thrust his hand down to his side to tap on the seat's armrest. Whether or not Flick liked his hair should be a moot point. They were friends. Best friends, despite not seeing each other for years. They'd kept in touch, with ripmails that had ebbed and flowed in frequency. More flowing in recent years as they put space between them and…that night.

That topic was there, always there, but never verbalized. What could they say? They were both adults with promising careers; they couldn't just derail that the night they graduated from the Academy. They'd done the only thing they could do: walk away and move on.

He was thinking too much again, and a vague hint of a headache brewed at his temples. Nothing significant, just a reminder of why he was stationed at Central and had been for the past couple of months. The lingering effects of a concussion meant he wasn't on Outrock Colony, on the edge of human space, for the last few months of his posting, and that meant taking leave and connecting with family—or friends—was an actual possibility. So he couldn't be too upset. Though next time, he'd try to arrange the downtime without the annoyance of an injury that was taking way too long to heal.

Finally the ship docked and Zed let the press of bodies eager to escape carry him along. As he approached the gate, he had a brief flash of panic that he wouldn't recognize Flick. Then he spotted familiar blond curls and a wide, welcoming smile and all of the worries melted away.

Zed grinned, his mouth stretching so wide it hurt. God, Flick looked good. Older (duh) and...damn, there was that bunch and lurch in his gut, the one he'd once ignored whenever he looked at his best friend. No more. Flick was hot, really hot, and Zed let himself appreciate that fact as he walked toward him.

He threw out his arms and engulfed Flick in a hug, squeezing hard. He opened his mouth to say something, but his tongue got tangled with everything he wanted to say. *I missed you, you look fantastic, I'm so happy to see you, I missed you, hugging you feels so good, how could I have walked away?*

Swallowing, he tried again. "Hi, you," he said, his voice rough.

"Hey," Flick said back, his voice muffled against Zed's chest. He sounded so casual, so nonchalant, as though this wasn't the first time they'd seen each other in forever. Had Zed miscalculated what this meeting would mean? Was this really just two old friends reuniting for a few days of fun to recapture their childhood, or—

Then he felt them. The trembles.

They quivered through Flick's body, small, slight, but there. He suddenly wanted to hold Flick tighter, closer, and make sure that he knew that no matter the distance between them, Zed would always be there for him.

Instead, when Flick tugged, Zed let him draw back.

"Should I be looking out for an angry farm wife?" Flick quipped.

Retreat. Regroup. Zed recognized that urge. Reluctantly, Zed pulled back from Flick, just enough so they weren't touching anymore, and adjusted the bag on his shoulder. "Not unless you decided you liked women, got married, and started a farm, all without telling me." Zed grinned, then turned his head to the side to display the still-angry scar. "Check it out."

"Damn, Zed. She could have cracked your skull."

"Yep." He looked back at Flick, his mouth twisting into a self-deprecating smile. "My first in-service scar, and it's from a bloody shovel. Christ."

He shook his head, then, still smiling, gestured for Flick to walk with him.

Felix scrubbed the back of his neck. "So, um, where did you book? I'm at the hostel."

"Oh. I, uh…didn't." He held Flick's gaze for a moment, then looked away. "I knew you were going to be here before me and I…well, I thought…I'd, uh, play it by ear." He looked at Flick again. His cheeks felt hot enough that they were probably glowing red. Dammit. He waved a hand and shook his head. "Regardless, you're not staying at a hostel on an Anatolius station when you're vacationing with an Anatolius. I'm sure they'll find a couple of rooms for us at the Olympus. Or, uh…" *Fuck, Zander, just say it.* "One room."

They didn't have to do anything. They could just talk all night. Fuck, he could even get a room with two beds. But none of that made it past Zed's dry throat and uncooperative tongue.

Flick stared at him and Zed thought for a moment that he'd fucked up. Again. Then, "One room would be good." A blush swept across Flick's cheeks, followed by a chuckle—which he quickly stifled. "Man, we are…ridiculous. I feel like I'm fourteen."

And just like that, they were kids again, best friends, without the elephant in the room looming over their shoulders. Not everything had to be decided now. Zed slung his arm across Flick's shoulders and directed him toward the Olympus. "Want me to see if they've got something with two twin beds so we can pretend we're back in the dorms?"

Flick's blush deepened, but he said nothing, just shook his head, and Zed let it go. Not everything had to be decided now, he reminded himself. But soon, they'd have to figure shit out.

Chapter Two

Felix could count on one hand the number of times he'd stayed in an actual hotel. In fact he only needed one finger. Normally, he saved credits by continuing to bunk aboard whatever ship he was assigned to while enjoying shore leave. Occasionally, he sprang for a hostel—when he thought he might need some privacy and a bunk not predisposed toward falling off of its hinges. Not that all his encounters over the past couple of years had taken place in a bed. In fact, he could probably count...

He needed to stop counting, and stop thinking about sex— which was really hard when faced with the largest bed in the galaxy. It was the size of an Olympic swimming pool and covered in a soft, puffy looking quilt and pillows thick enough to plug a hull breach. About six hundred of them.

Felix looked at Zed instead and felt yet another blush sting its way down from his scalp and across his cheeks, where it met the one springing up from his neck. Damn his pale skin, and damn Zed for being so fucking hot. He was melting Felix's synapses. Conversation as they crossed the station to collect his hold-all from the hostel had been weird and stilted. Felix had expected it to take some time for them to reconnect. He hadn't expected the odd combination of strangeness and familiarity, though, as if someone had presented him with an imperfect copy of the Zed he'd grown up with. One more gorgeous, just as personable, well-versed in their personal history, but somehow different. Unknowable.

"There's only one bed," Felix said.

Zed's brows crooked together. Man, he looked good. Felix preferred Zed's dark brown hair longer, but the shorter cut made his steely blue eyes huge and...had his cheekbones always been so prominent? His mouth, Felix remembered. Wide, with full lips. The straight nose, those dark and mobile brows.

"It was going to be a bit of a wait for two and the beds at these hotels are always huge. Is it a problem?" Zed finally answered.

Felix's answering shrug was more reflex than planned. "It's the size of a basketball court, I think we'll be fine."

"You still like basketball?"

"Yeah. I don't get to watch it much. Mostly old replays we pick up through rip comms."

Felix glanced at the bed. They could sleep together there for a week and not bump into one another. It'd be fine. Unless Zed had planned for them to do some bumping. Was that why he'd decided not to wait for a bigger room?

Jesus. He really needed to stop staring at the bed.

Backing away, Felix swung his hold-all from his shoulder and dropped it onto the floor. Without looking at Zed, he angled toward the door on the far side, what he hoped would be the bathroom.

Zed caught his arm as he passed. "Hold up."

Felix stopped.

"I can get us a different room if the bed is a problem."

"Forget the bed."

Zed's brows dipped low. "Do you want your own room?"

"No. What I want is to take a leak."

"Oh." Zed let go.

Zed was still standing at the end of the bed when Felix finished inspecting every corner of the palatial bathroom and had washed his hands four times. Soap smelled good. Sorta like Zed. All woodsy with a hint of citrus.

"Do you want to get two rooms?" Felix asked.

"What I want is for this to not be so weird."

"Yeah, I know. But it's been four years." Felix scratched the side of his head, catching the scent of sandalwood and lemon as his hand passed his face. "It didn't occur to me until that last week at school that it'd be that long. Two years, four, whatever.

Seemed unreal, you know? Like we'd probably bump into each other out there somewhere. After training if not before."

Zed's smile had a slightly distant quality.

Dropping his hand, Felix went to inspect the mini bar. Maybe they should fall back to Plan B. That'd been the one where he lined up shot glasses, right? Or got drunk? As he studied the line of bottles—no mini versions for VIP guests!—he realized he didn't want to waste any of the little time he had with Zed by getting drunk. He wanted to remember these five days. They might be all he had for the next who knew however long.

Zed still hadn't moved when Felix turned around again. Had he said something wrong? Felix pushed out a sigh. "Okay, here it is. I'm not expecting anything, all right? I'm not going to throw myself at your feet and tell you I love you and ask you to promise me the next four years. I'm over it. Took me a long time, I know, and I'm sorry for any ripmails I didn't answer, and for the fact I've let a few queue up lately. We were in the—"

Registering the fact Zed now had a strange look on his face, Felix clamped his mouth shut, cutting his apology off at the knees. Fuck. He *had* said something wrong. But which part? And why was Zed so quiet?

Zed had dropped his bag on a proper stand thing in the corner of the bedroom. He walked over to it and thumbed the release. The bag softened and fell open, displaying two stacks of neatly folded clothing. "How about if we head out?" he said, lifting the top two layers away to get at something underneath. "Get something to eat, a drink. Find some music or a show." He glanced up. "Do something that isn't us staring at the big bed in the middle of the room, wondering if we're going to sleep on separate sides or in the middle."

Felix's thoughts wandered to the middle of the bed, to what they might do there in between banked clouds of pillows and linen. Was that what Zed wanted? Did he want to sleep—or not sleep—in the middle? The fact they only had a limited amount of time could be the pass Zed needed. Five days to fuck and then...no, Zed wouldn't forget. If not only because he knew Felix wouldn't, despite the brave speech he'd just given.

"Felix."

At the sound of his name, Felix returned to the conversation to find Zed standing right in front of him. This close, he caught a whiff of the familiar and strange that had so far dogged their afternoon. Zed's aftershave and the chemical tang of reprocessed air. This close, he could appreciate, again, how large his best friend was. Broad across the shoulders and half a head taller. Zed leaned in and brushed their lips together. A kiss that didn't feel like a kiss, but a touch that could be nothing else.

"Stop thinking so hard," he said, his breath tickling Felix's stunned lips. "That's my job. Now go put on a clean shirt." Stepping back, he cocked his head. Eyes twinkling now. "You did bring a change of clothes, didn't you?"

"Yeah."

"Forward march, soldier."

Why hadn't he just waited for a room with two beds? Flick was clearly embarrassed by Zed's assumptions—and now, so was Zed. Flick couldn't have made it clearer that he wasn't interested in pursuing anything of a romantic nature.

He really should have called down and asked for them to be moved to a new room. But fleeing the scene of the crime seemed like a better proposition at the time. And it had led them here, to a laser tag arena, so that couldn't be all bad, right? They were up against a trio of teenagers—spoiled rich kids, by the looks of them, and Zed would know. He and Flick had won the first round, and now a couple of unintelligible shouts drifted from the other team's camp. Trash talk.

Flick rolled his eyes. "You know," he yelled over the barricade, "if you're gonna be smart-asses, you should at least enunciate!"

"Bite! Me!" The words were very clear and perfectly pronounced.

"You told them to enunciate." Zed chuckled. "How's the charge on your rifle?"

"More than enough to take out these two dickwads."

"Remember, they're just kids."

"Not anymore, they're not." Flick's eyes glittered with a mix of amusement and ferocity. "Now they're the enemy."

The siren sounded to start the second round. Zed shared a grin with Flick, bumped fists, and headed off to flank the so-called enemy. If they won this round, too, they'd get new opponents—theoretically, they could keep going all day on the one admission fee, if they kept racking up the victories. Not that he was worried about the cost. It was more the principle of the thing. Bragging rights. It felt like he and Flick were back at the Academy, taking on all comers and kicking—

Zed's stomach lurched as his feet left the floor. Instantly he snapped into officer mode, assessing the situation. Was the gravity loss throughout the station or—

Just as quickly as it disappeared, gravity came back on and reinforced its hold. Harshly. Zed slammed to the plasmix floor and rolled, distributing the brunt of the fall. From a pained groan off the in the direction he'd left Flick, someone else hadn't been so agile.

Forgetting all about the game, he sprinted across the battleground. A laser shot stung his shoulder—a fleeting sensation designed to inform but not harm. He lifted a finger in the universal sign for fuck you, then skidded to a stop beside Flick, who was sitting against one of the strategically placed barricades, blood streaming down his face from his nose.

"'M okay, 'm okay," he muttered as Zed knelt beside him.

"Shit." Zed peeled off his shirt and folded it up to press against Flick's nose. "Can you breathe okay?" Eying the other side of the battleground, Zed shouted, "We forfeit!"

Cheers erupted. Assholes. Scowling, Zed pulled out his wallet and punched a couple of holographic buttons to officially end the match. Oh look, there was a button for medical assistance. Zed pressed it, then put his wallet away and turned back to Flick.

"Here, keep pressure on it." Zed cupped the back of Flick's head and pressed the blood-soaked cloth more firmly to his nose.

"Ow!"

Zed winced. "Sorry."

"You could've warned me that the laser tag had zero-g mode." The words came out of Flick's mouth sounding muffled and garbled, but Zed figured them out.

"I didn't know. I thought I'd picked a standard battleground."

He backed off as a couple of attendants appeared with a first aid kit. Shortly thereafter, an older man wearing a suit marched up their three former opponents. He looked about as impressed as Zed.

"Mr. Anatolius, I'm Greg Hoffelder, the director of Hemera Laser Fun. I'm sorry to meet you like this, but I wanted to share that we registered the momentary loss of gravity in your match and were able to trace it back to your opponents." Greg leveled a glare at the teenagers.

Zed's brows rose. "You hacked the match?"

The boy in the middle—and he was definitely a boy still, with zits and limbs too gangly for his body—crossed his arms and looked like he wanted to be anywhere else. "Yeah. But we were never gonna win against you guys and—"

"Shut up, Mario!" one of the other boys growled.

"And now we're banned for a month. Jeez." The third boy glared at Zed. "*Everyone* knows that the grav is fair game for hacking."

"We didn't. Ow, fuck." Flick pushed at the attendant's fingers until she moved her hands away from his face. "I think it's stopped bleeding. What do you think, is it broken?"

Zed waited for the attendant to move away, then, gently palpitated the bloodstained flesh. "Nah, I think it's good. How's it feel?"

"Like shit." Flick made an experimental sniff and flinched. "Damn it, that hurts."

The game attendants produced an icepack—one of the ones Zed was familiar with from exercises, where you just had to break the material inside the plasmix to get the reverse thermal reaction to occur. The thing went super cold in seconds. Zed pressed it gently to Flick's face and Flick hissed.

"I'm sorry," he murmured.

Flick made a grunting noise that might have been acceptance of the apology or dismissal, Zed couldn't tell.

"This whole...none of this is going as I'd planned." Zed sighed.

Flick looked up at Zed for a few seconds, his gaze unreadable. "Maybe that's the problem."

"What?"

"The plan part of things." He shrugged and winced again as the icepack moved. "Maybe we need to toss the plan. Start new."

Zed frowned. "I don't want to pretend we don't know each other. Or that we didn't—"

Flick held up a hand to stop Zed. "We're not the same guys we were at eighteen. I think expecting that we could just pick up where we left off..."

Goddamn it. Zed let go of the icepack. Flick was holding onto it with one hand anyway, and Zed couldn't be touching him when...when... "Do you want to cancel our—"

"No!" Flick shouted, then cleared his throat. "No," he said more calmly. "But let's...just play it by ear. I mean, this was a good start."

"In theory," Zed said, his lips twisting into a grimace.

"In theory," Flick agreed.

Zed sucked on his teeth for a moment, debating with himself. "Do you want another room?" he finally asked.

It took Flick just as long to answer. "No," he said quietly.

"Okay." Zed tried to ignore the flutters of triumph in his stomach. "Let's go get room service and see if we can find a bad holo to watch."

"Or a basketball game?" Flick suggested hopefully.

"Sure." It didn't matter to Zed—as long as they were together.

Jumping hurt. He had to remember that. But the Titans needed this point to take the game from the Ancients. The plush carpet of the Anatolius suite was not thick enough to cushion Felix's landing, though. Pain shot from the base of his jaw, up through the bridge of his nose, where it poked directly into the back of his skull. "Jesus, Joseph and Mary."

"You okay?" Zed pulled Felix's hands from his face. "Don't touch your nose, you'll make it worse."

"Don't see how," Felix mumbled.

"Maybe let the Titans shoot the rest of their baskets themselves?"

"They need my help, man. They need this game for a chance at the quarter finals." Zed was laughing quietly. Felix pushed him backward by shoving a hand into his shoulder, but found he couldn't help laughing as well. "Hey, this is the first live game I've seen in two years. If I'm gonna help my team, now's the time."

"I'd forgotten how much you like basketball."

"And I'd forgotten how much you like to eat." Food crowded the low table in front of the sofa. One of everything from the room service menu.

Felix perched on the edge of the sofa and leaned forward to grab another strawberry by the stem. He tipped his head back and dangled it over his lips, teasing the pointed end with his tongue, absently, liking the texture, before taking a bite. Juice ran from the corner of his mouth and he swiped his tongue sideways to catch it. Having glanced in the same direction, he caught Zed staring at him—eyes heavy lidded, lips parted. Cheeks flushing, Felix looked back at his strawberry. The mischief maker within suggested he stick his tongue into the little hollow inside the fruit. Moan a little, then suck the strawberry into his mouth. Zed wouldn't be the only one turned on by the tease, though, and they hadn't actually decided if they were going to revisit old territory or not. But, really, could something like that be initiated by a conversation?

Fuck it.

Closing his eyes, he stuck his tongue into the strawberry. Zed's sharp intake of breath would have been audible back on Earth. The sound—the urgency of it, the want transmitted by that one quick inhale—shot straight to Felix's groin. The strawberry was sweet and warm. He sucked juice from the middle before wrapping his lips around the rest of the fruit and drawing it into his mouth. Cheering erupted from the large holo screen flickering in front of them. Someone had scored a point—maybe even his beloved Titans. The short, quiet panting next to him seemed louder. Definitely more significant. Felix finished chewing, swallowed, opened his eyes and turned to face Zed, who looked as though he'd come in his pants. Or was about to.

"Holy shit." Zed pulled at his pants, obviously needing to rearrange certain folds of fabric.

It was so hard not to look at his crotch.

"I don't know whether to feed you more strawberries, push you back into the couch or just yell at you for giving me a hard on."

Well, that was frank.

Chuckling, Felix reached for another strawberry.

"Wait." Zed's hand arrested his, callused fingertips grazing Felix's knuckles. "Hold up. Before you drive us both insane…maybe we could just talk a while? That's what we haven't done, you know."

Felix swallowed. "Talk about what?" Did Zed want to make a new plan, or outline some rules for whatever happened next?

"Just stuff. All we've done since we got here is stare at a bed, nearly get your nose broken and watch a basketball game." He moved his hand away from Felix's, holding it up in a placating gesture. "What I mean is… You were right. I had a plan and it didn't include you eating strawberries."

Grinning, Felix picked up another strawberry and twirled the stem, making the small red fruit spin.

Zed groaned. "Jesus, Flick."

Felix popped the strawberry into his mouth without a tease and flopped back into the couch. "Okay, you want to talk? Tell me what you've been up to on Central. Your last couple of ripcomms were really vague."

"Anything out of Central gets sniffed and snipped, you know that."

Especially anything transmitted from the AEF Headquarters. Felix had supposed a post at the seat of human government would suit Zed, but now he could tell it didn't.

"How long are you going to be stuck there?" he asked.

"I don't know. I've been...looking into other postings."

"Yeah? Like where?"

Zed short of shrugged, sort of frowned. "I don't want to talk about work."

Felix chuckled. "We're soldiers. Our work is our life. It's all we have to talk about."

"You get any time to tinker aboard the *McCandless*?"

"Not really..." Felix thought over the numbing routine that was life aboard a battle cruiser. "I did devise a new locking mechanism for the aft evaporator storage."

"Because..."

"Not many private places aboard a battlecruiser."

"Oh." Zed's expression darkened. He rubbed the back of his hand across his mouth. "Need privacy a lot?"

"Not often." He had a casual something going with one of the guys on his crew. Very casual. So casual, it was more like coincidence. "How 'bout you?"

Zed's hand migrated to the back of his head. His new scar. "My head is still ringing." He gave a wry smile.

"So...with all the important work you're doing at Central..." Paper pushing. He'd be scanning holo reports and making reports of what he'd read for other benched soldiers to scan. "Have you kept up with your music?" That had always been Zed's main hobby. Weird instrumental compositions made using a couple of different wallet programs. Felix didn't understand Zed's music, but he liked it—mostly because it represented a part of his friend few people ever saw. What he was like beneath the handsome exterior wrapped in a layer of perfect soldier. It was Zed the dreamer, the gentle idealist. The man who would one day be a hero to more than just Felix Ingesson.

Zed had his hand on his pocket. "Well, I did do this thing..." Cheeks flushing, he moved his hand away. "It's not really—"

"I want to hear it."

Zed fiddled with the fabric of his pocket. "It's not finished yet."

"I don't care. Besides, who else are you going to play it for?"

Felix held his breath as he waited for Zed to answer, suddenly and keenly aware that if there was someone else—outside of Zed's brothers—who got to hear his music, then Felix would no longer be...privileged? Special? The best friend.

Just as he thought to suggest Zed needn't answer, Zed pulled his wallet out and folded it open. He glanced up at Felix. "Besides you, Brennan and Maddox?" His smile was wistful. "No one. You know that."

Felix let out a breath. Unsure how capture the precious feeling imparted by Zed's statement, he ate another strawberry while Zed fiddled with a holo display.

The music caught him by surprise, as it always did. Haunting melodies strung together with beautiful phrases. If Felix were to try and make music, his compositions would be mathematical. Methodical. Zed's music wasn't chaotic, but veered as close as it could to the edge of sense, combining rhythms that shouldn't work together but did. The melody...traveled, rarely visiting the same place twice, but beneath, there was a constant. Felix couldn't figure out just what it was, couldn't pin it down, but there was a note, or a beat that tied it all together.

When the piece ended, Zed eyed him cautiously. "What did you think?"

Felix didn't know what to say until his memory suddenly snapped the pieces of what he'd just heard together. "It's...it's a story, isn't it?"

Zed immediately brightened. "Yeah."

"That's what all your music is, right?"

Rather than look offended by the fact Felix had only just got it, some ten years after he'd heard Zed's first mournful tune, he simply nodded. "Mostly. Sometimes it's just me playing with sound, but I always have a sort of picture in mind."

"Tell me about the picture for this one."

He'd thought Zed might hesitate and he seemed to, for the space of a breath. Then he launched into a tale—him among the stars, searching—and Felix fell into listening. He was interested in the story, but really, Zed could be describing the food laid out across the coffee table. Just to hear him talk, passionately and animatedly. This was what had been missing so far. Zed being Zed. Felix laid his head back on the couch and closed his eyes, prepared to listen until Zed ran out of words.

Chapter Three

He was back on the rooftop with Flick, watching the fireworks and holos spell out their names overhead, along with those of the rest of the graduating class. Zed knew it was a dream—a lucid dream, maybe, because he could smell Flick's wonderful scent, the one he hadn't known he'd miss until he didn't catch a whiff of it every day. The tang that reminded Zed of a space station, and circuits, the perfect embodiment of Flick.

They were curled up on the roof—which was much more comfortable than it had been in real life, thank you dreamland—Flick's back to his chest, Zed's arms wrapped around him and holding him close. The unseen fireworks overhead cast Flick's blonde hair in various shades of red and orange and blue and purple that Zed was almost too close to see.

"Gonna miss you," he whispered.

It was a memory, but not—on some level, Zed knew this wasn't quite how that last night had happened, but it didn't matter. One of his hands skimmed downward, slipping under the waistband of Flick's underwear. His groan as he found Flick's rock-hard erection rivalled Flick's.

They hadn't been together enough times for Zed to know what Flick liked, so he improvised. Whatever made Flick squirm and groan and grunt was a good thing—especially when he started rocking back against Zed. God, yes. Zed met each thrust with a press forward of his hips, rutting his cock into the perfect groove of Flick's covered ass. He tucked his face into the crook of Flick's neck and shoulder and breathed in his tangy scent, now overlaid with musk and lust. His thumb swept over the tip of Flick's cock, spreading the warm bead of liquid there all over the head, which only made Flick's movements more frenzied, more desperate.

God, so good. So fucking good. Zed licked the bare skin of Flick's shoulder, not even wondering at Flick's lack of clothing—dreams were dreams.

"Zed, don't stop. Don't."

"Can't," Zed agreed, his voice shaking.

Wait...

He blinked and the rooftop faded away, leaving a bed. A hotel room. Synthesized morning light filtering through the polarized windows. Flick shaking in his arms. Zed's balls drawn up and ready—

"Fuck," Flick groaned, the curse long, drawn-out, as he stilled for a second, then thrust again. Warmth rushed over Zed's hand, the smell of come and lust intensifying, and even though Zed knew he wasn't dreaming, knew he'd accidentally crossed a line, he couldn't hold back. With a gasp and a cry, he pressed harder into Flick's backside and froze as his orgasm overpowered him.

The bliss fled way too quickly, leaving Zed with a hand covered in cooling jizz and boxers full of the same—and a suspicion that whatever progress he and Flick had made yesterday had been rubbed out along with his morning wood.

"Sorry," he whispered. "Fuck, I'm really sorry."

Flick let out a noise that might have been a sigh or a gentle laugh—it was hard to tell with him facing away from Zed. "Good dream?"

Awkward. "You were in it, so, um...yeah." He pulled away, trying to move so he didn't smear his messy hand anywhere. "So much for staying on my side of the bed. Shit," he muttered, pushing to his feet. "Look, I'll...I'll get you another room, okay?"

"Stop with the room shit. We dealt with that yesterday." Flick rolled over to glare at him.

"Yeah. Before..." Zed waggled his come-covered fingers.

"It was a sleepy hand job. One step above a wet dream." Flick held Zed's gaze, his own hazel eyes unreadable. "Do you hear me complaining?"

No, but that didn't help the shame currently cascading through Zed. He shifted uncomfortably from foot to foot. "I'm gonna…" He waved at the bathroom.

Flick opened his mouth as if he was going to say something—then closed it, giving a little headshake. "Yeah, okay. Go."

Released from standing there like an idiot, Zed bee-lined for the shower, eager to put this new disaster behind him.

Felix listened to Zed moving around the bathroom. The thick walls of the suite muted the sounds of his progress, but determined attention won through. Felix would rather listen to Zed washing his hands than contemplate what had just happened.

Zed stopped moving after he finished at the sink.

The memory of Zed's body rocking into him slid into the quiet pause. The hard point of Zed cock pushing at the crease of his ass, the rough-smooth texture of Zed's hand over his dick. The pressure of his thumb, the maddening twist every time he pulled up. It'd been the best hand job Felix had ever received—probably because he'd been able to smell Zed's sleep-warm skin, and the fingers wrapped around his shaft had been both familiar and strange.

The best part had been how natural it felt. Right. Inevitable? Felix had been aware of Zed most of the night, his quite breaths, the little shifts as he rolled from time to time. He'd woken a little when Zed moved up behind him and cuddled. What else to do but snuggle backward, let the heat of Zed's chest move through his back and into his chest. Into his heart.

In the bathroom, Zed still hadn't moved—unless he'd figured out how to shower like a ninja.

Two choices floated about on the taste of morning breath. Felix could let Zed shower alone, which would lead to Felix also probably showering alone. Awkward showers would be followed by an uncomfortable breakfast and a day filled with avoiding the fact their hips had moved perfectly in time. After a number of years and a handful of other lovers, they'd fallen into a matched rhythm with nary a hitch. Felix generally didn't bottom, but had

Zed had lube handy, he'd have lost his underwear so fast the fiber might combusted with the friction.

Was Zed a top? He had the whole gruff alpha thing going.

Focus, Felix.

He pushed back the covers and scrambled to the edge of the stupidly wide bed, second choice decided upon before he'd fully examined it. Fuck awkward, and fuck plans. If Zed didn't want this, this was his chance to say so. Felix didn't know how they'd make it work, or if they even could. Hell, they might only have these five days—the four remaining. If that was it, then that was it. Seize the day and all that.

His heart jerked around in his chest as he approached the bathroom. A sharp pain across his left palm cautioned him to uncurl his fingers. He stopped in front of the door and looked at his hand. A row of red crescents marked the skin. Maybe he should default back to option one.

His marked up hand had already palmed the door panel, though, and it slid back without remorse to reveal Zed doing exactly what Felix had pictured. He stood by the sink, hands braced against the sides, and looked in the mirror. His boxers were in a heap on the floor and...

All the moisture evaporated from Felix's mouth. Specialist training and two years out in the field had stripped the last softness from Zed's frame. He was still generously proportioned—wide shoulders, powerful arms and legs, firm, ripe buttocks. Shoulders bulging with musculature, rounded pecs and a hard, flat abdomen. There was nothing extra, though. His hips were trim, his legs long and lean. His ass. Felix couldn't lift his gaze from Zed's ass. He knew if he looked a little sideways, he'd catch a glimpse of Zed's cock, but his ass...

"Do you need the head?"

Felix had a feeling Zed had spoken more than once. He'd heard words, but hadn't made sense of them. He looked up. "Huh?"

"Do you need..." Zed gestured the toilet.

"No." Actually, yes, but the vague pressure in his bladder wasn't the reason he'd come into the bathroom. He'd wanted to—what had he been going to do?

Zed made an impatient noise, calling Felix to focus.

"I want to talk," Felix said.

"Can't it wait until I've had a shower?"

"No." Felix moved into the bathroom, into the heady sphere of Zed's naked influence. Holy mother of everything. "God, it's hard to focus on anything with you naked."

"Want to get to the point?"

The sharpness of Zed's tone cut exactly to that, the point. Felix tore his gaze away from naked flesh and looked into Zed's steel blue eyes. "This morning—what happened in bed. Do you regret it?"

"Why?"

Why? Was that some interrogation technique? Get Felix to answer all the questions so Zed didn't have to? Fine.

"Because I don't." Felix held up a hand, forestalling any response from Zed. "It felt damn good and I want to do it again, other way 'round. I want to spend all day in bed with you. I know it can't go anywhere, that these few days are all we're likely to get, but..." He swallowed. "I'm good with that." He wasn't, but he could stretch a lie over a few days and mourn the bastard afterward. "We fit, Zed. It works between us. We could, I dunno, make it about the physical if you like. I know you want me. Why not let yourself have me? Just for today, or the days we have left."

There it was, the proverbial carrot held out for Zed to grab. Flick wasn't even trying to keep it out of his grasp, not anymore—and that pissed Zed off.

"Goddamn it, Flick, you think this is just physical?" He pushed away from the sink and, movements sharp and jerky with temper, turned on the water in the shower. It gave him something to do, something to look at. Something to act as a buffer between him and the guy he'd just...*fuck*...molested while half asleep.

Gritting his teeth, he stepped under the water, not caring that it wasn't the right temperature yet.

Flick grumbled, words Zed couldn't decipher over the rush of water—then the shower door opened and Flick stepped inside. "No, it's not just physical, asshole. Never has been."

Zed swiped water away from his eyes. "Then why would you even say that?"

Flick turned on the other showerhead—wouldn't be an Anatolius suite without that luxury—then crossed his arms and glared at Zed. "Why do you think?"

They shared a hard stare, one that reminded Zed of when they were kids and neither wanted to back down from an argument. But they weren't kids anymore. Zed rubbed the scar on the back of his head and let out a breath.

"'Cause we're both scared." He held Flick's gaze, noticing that it softened a bit with that admission out in the air between them. "Can I tell you what I had planned? Coming here?"

God, this was frightening. More frightening than seeing his lover's wife lift up that shovel with murder in her eyes.

Flick sluiced water away from his face, and Zed reflected that this was not how he'd pictured having this conversation—naked and wet would be a better choice for more fun activities. But, whatever, he'd take it. "Yeah, okay," Flick said, his voice just audible over the soft rumble of the shower.

Time to jump. Zed had no idea if he had a parachute on or not.

"I love you." He held up a hand to stop Flick from saying anything. "Just let me talk for a minute, okay?" He drew in a shaky breath. "I figured it out that night."

"Graduation night? And you didn't—"

"I didn't. Leaving you was hard enough. The timing wasn't right—you know it wasn't right."

Flick turned his face away from Zed, his jaw tight. Fuck, fuck, fuck. Zed continued on.

"So, my plan was to see you, now, see if there was a spark beyond friendship and—" Another trembling breath. "If there was, I wanted to talk to you about putting in for a joint posting somewhere."

Flick's gaze snapped back to Zed's. "Joint posting? You mean stationed together?"

"Yeah. It's probably not really an option right yet, and I don't want to rush us into anything. So…maybe not a true joint posting, but we could try to angle for ones that are closer than you on the *McCandless* and me at the edge of human space. Or at Central. There's got to be a happy medium somewhere, right?"

Flick tilted his head, looking at Zed like he was a particularly interesting—and broken—engine part. The silence spun out between them and Zed adjusted the water temperature, and then the intensity and pattern of the stream, just for something to do.

Flick huffed out an impatient breath. "What are you trying to say?"

Zed suddenly found the interface for the shower really interesting. "Look, I know you already said you were over what happened on graduation night. I get it, I do. But I thought…I'd just put it out there. In case… But if there isn't any chance, then I'll have to live with it, right? Because really, I'm the one who fucked it—"

"Yeah, you did."

Zed dared a glance at Flick. "I regret walking away without making you a promise. I thought—I wasn't sure. It was such a new thing and—" He shook his head, looking back to the shower controls. "I want to try. I want to be yours, you to be mine. Boyfriends."

Chapter Four

Boyfriends. After walking away from him—without looking back—Zed wanted to be boyfriends. Loved him, apparently. Had loved him for four goddamned years. Had told Felix to pick his heart up off that rooftop graduation night and put it back in his chest, knowing he carried it with him when he left. Knowing Felix would pine for him.

Had Zed loved him while he was boning his colonial farmer?

Had Zed loved him while he was pictured all over the society nets with Riley Whatsherface?

His fist connected with Zed's face with almost no conscious effort on Felix's part. Zed rocked back, eyes wide with shock, a hand coming up to cup the angry red mark blooming along his jaw. Felix turned so fast, he slid across the tile. He grabbed the door. Then, finding his balance, he pushed it open and stepped carefully across the bathroom floor until he reached the towel rail. They should have done this in the bedroom where soft linens and the funk of sex...

Felix growled, the sound well suited to all he felt inside. He was being chewed up.

"What the fuck?" Zed stepped carefully out of the shower.

"Four years!" He yanked at a towel, not quite sure if he was more angry or hurt or just confused. "Did it take you that long to decide you loved me, or did you just need to test out a few other folks first? Make sure I was the hole that fit best?"

"That is not fucking fair."

"No? What do you think I've been doing all this time, huh? Waiting in a box for you to unwrap when you were ready?"

"Of course not. Flick—"

"Don't call me that!"

Zed looked as if he'd swallowed something sharp. "Felix."

Felix left the bathroom before he could hit Zed again—not that he had the strength for it. He felt sapped, weak. He also felt as though he might cry. He flung his towel across the bed and rummaged in his hold-all for clean clothes. He'd got his undershorts on when two strong arms caught him from behind. Annoyed he hadn't heard Zed's approach, Felix kicked and struggled. Zed's hold didn't loosen—but nor did it tighten.

"Stop, please. Just—"

"What are you doing?" Felix asked.

"Will you just listen to me?"

"I don't want to."

"You're acting like a child."

"You broke my heart, Zed. How did you expect me to act?"

Zed's arms loosened, then fell away. "I…what?"

Felix turned around. "I told you I loved you and you walked away. How did you think I was going to feel?"

"I wasn't ready."

Felix opened his mouth, retort ready to roll…and breathed out nothing but air. He'd said almost those exact words to someone else. Someone who had loved him, who might have been prepared to wait for him. Someone he hadn't been able to commit to because of the man standing in front of him right now.

Zed wasn't the only one who'd been looking for the right fit. Felix had had a fairly seriously relationship with that close friend in specialist training and he'd tried to love Theo as much as he could tell Theo loved him. He'd almost succeeded, too, until he remembered they'd be separated by the same thing that had torn him and Zed apart. He and Theo wouldn't be stationed together. Not so early in their careers—maybe not ever.

"Fuck," he whispered.

Now truly deflated, he sat on the end of the bed. Zed sat next to him and Felix noticed he'd wrapped a towel around his hips. His skin—as golden as Felix remembered—glistened with moisture. The scent of soap and Zed wafted around them. Felix massaged his chest, right over his heart—which didn't seem to be with the program. It beat solidly and slowly, as if he hadn't just thrown an epic shit fit and hit the man he…

"It hurt," he said, glancing sideways.

Zed's steel blue eyes showed remorse. "I'm sorry."

Felix nodded. He should apologize for the bruise creeping along Zed's jaw, but he didn't feel like it. Instead, he rejoined the conversation Zed had wanted to have in the shower of all places. Had he meant it? Zed would never lie. The better question would be did he know what he really wanted. Of course he did. Zed planned everything.

"You knew. Yesterday, you knew this was what you wanted."

"Yeah."

"Did you know I'd hit you?"

Zed prodded his jaw...gently, but one corner of his mouth twitched. "I should have guessed."

Was this the part where Felix should say he was sorry, or lay out the truth? Maybe the latter could serve as the former. "I lied before. I'm not over you." The pain in his chest sharpened for a second. "I really want to hate you, Zed." No, he didn't. Never that. His breath hitched. "I mean..."

"Shh. I know what you mean."

Zed leaned toward him and Felix met him halfway. Not for a kiss—they weren't acting out some romance holovid. Their shoulders touched and seemed to meld together, and the simple connection felt like a combination of support and complicity. After a moment, Zed shifted so he could bring his arm up around Felix's back. Felix turned into the sideways embrace and put his arms around Zed's waist. Tucked his face in under Zed's chin and hugged him tight.

"I'm sorry," Zed whispered. "It was so new and...I didn't trust it. I didn't trust *me*."

"Couldn't you trust me?" Flick muttered into Zed's chest.

"I should have."

"Damn straight."

"I didn't mean to break your heart." Zed brushed a hand over Flick's wet curls. The words, maybe the gesture, elicited only a grunt. "The timing was…"

"It sucked," Flick supplied as Zed's voice drifted into silence.

"Yeah."

"No matter what you said about arranging postings and shit, the timing still sucks." Flick lifted his head to eye Zed. "Why now?"

He could say he was older and wiser, but though the *older* part fit, the *wiser* sure didn't. The scar on the back of his head was a reminder of just how wise he wasn't. "I love being in the AEF. I loved being focused on my career. Anyone I've been with—I was with them because they didn't interfere with that focus. They might have been fun company, someone to spend downtime with, but they didn't matter. Not like a partner should. And then I was laid up for a few days, where I couldn't watch a holo or read or really do anything but think."

"You must have been in heaven," Flick said drily.

Yeah, his penchant for deep thinking had been well known amongst his friends at the Academy. "Not really." He sighed. "Look, what I'm trying to say is that my focus shifted. Less about the job and more about what I left behind. Who."

"Me."

"Yeah."

"And you really think we can make this work?"

"I want to try." Zed held Flick's gaze. "I'm ready to try."

He left the question unspoken, but it hovered in the air between them anyway.

Are you?

In answer, Flick pushed up and caught Zed's mouth with his. The first kiss was gentle—almost hesitant. The second less so— but it wasn't bruising or punishing, either. Just…forceful. As if it had waited years to be unleashed. Zed opened his mouth and welcomed the invasion. Needing it. Wanting it. Warmth rushed through him at the realization that even if their future was balanced on the weight of a *yes* or a *no* from Flick, they would still have this.

He let Flick push him back onto the bed. His towel opened and fell away, and Zed wasn't sure if it had been helped by Flick's clever fingers or merely movement and gravity. He scooted back, his neck arched to keep his lips in contact with Flick's as they moved to the center of the massive bed, and ignored the twinge from the bruise on his jaw. This moment was worth the pain of a hundred bruises.

Somehow, Flick managed to wiggle out of his undershorts. When the full length of his body pressed Zed into the mattress, it was free of any clothing. Nothing separated them. Skin on hot skin, a sensation Zed had dreamed of feeling with this man in particular, but had worried he never would. He gasped as their cocks came in contact and immediately gave a thrust upward, wanting more. But kissing was too important, too *needed*, to just stop. The connection of lips on lips was deceptively simple— never before had Zed understood just how essential it could be.

Flick moaned into his mouth and his hips took up the motion Zed's had insisted on. His cock slid in the groove that separated Zed's abdomen from his thigh, as though it had been made for that specific purpose. And it was good, so good, but Zed wanted more. With an effort, he braced a hand on Flick's chest and tried to separate their mouths. It took a couple of tries before he could resist the siren call of Flick's swollen, reddened lips and form words.

"Wait."

"Hmm?" Flick's buttocks flexed and Zed almost—*almost*— groaned and fell back into pure sensation.

Fuck. What was he going to ask? Oh yeah. "I want to make love."

"Isn't this—"

"You inside me."

That got Flick's attention. He froze and pushed back just enough to stare down at Zed, his eyes searching for...something. "Do you mean...you want to...Really?" he finally managed.

Zed swallowed and nodded.

"Have you ever....?"

Zed shook his head.

This time, the shudder went through Flick's body. He leaned forward, his forehead resting on Zed's. "Okay...fuck. Okay."

"Do you prefer to—"

"I prefer to do exactly what we're gonna do." Flick chuckled and lifted his head. The laughter faded quickly, replaced by heat. "I'm gonna make it so good. I promise."

"I trust you." And he did—with every particle of his being.

Flick found lube in the nightstand drawer. He didn't ask about it, but the fact that he found it without Zed directing him to it said he remembered Zed's need to plan and be prepared. There might be years separating them now, new experiences, but they were still them. Zed and Felix. Best friends and now...

Zed hissed at the feel of slick fingers down below. It wasn't like he'd never touched himself there—he just had never shared it with anyone.

"You okay?"

"Don't stop," Zed ordered, forcing himself to relax.

Another stroke of a finger, then it sank inside. Zed groaned.

"Can't believe you've never..." Flick's finger wiggled, then another joined it. The burn was unfamiliar...but good, in a weird sort of way.

Zed brushed his fingers against Flick's cheek, encouraging him to look up. "No one else ever mattered enough."

Flick whispered something—might have been a curse—and crooked his fingers. Zed jolted with the shock of overwhelming intensity. His cock bobbed against his lower abdomen for a second before Flick bent forward and engulfed the leaking head in his mouth.

"Christ!" Zed pushed his head back into the mattress, trying to find enough willpower not to come. His hips rocked, pushing his dick up into that warm cave of a mouth, and back onto those amazing fingers. He'd never felt anything quite like it—all encompassing. His movements quickened, beyond his control, and he nearly whimpered when Flick released his cock with a pop.

"I've got you," Flick murmured. He pulled over a pillow and tucked it under the small of Zed's back, then positioned himself over Zed, moving his hands to either side of Zed's torso to brace himself. "Better to be on your stomach for the first time, you know."

"Want this. Want to see you." Zed gripped Flick's ribs and tugged him forward. "C'mon."

Flick looked down and gripped his cock to line himself up, then lifted his gaze to watch Zed's face. "Tell me if you want me to stop, if you want to change positions, or—"

"Felix, *please*."

A little growl escaped as Flick gave in and pressed forward. Zed held his breath at the sensation of something that felt really fucking big pressing at a hole that was really fucking small, but Flick didn't stop. He kept moving, pressing, demanding that Zed's body allow him that intimacy that he'd never allowed anyone else. He slipped inside, millimeter by millimeter, and damn, it hurt. Zed's erection flagged.

"Gets better," Flick said, his voice strained. "Fuck, you're tight."

Zed focused on breathing, on relaxing muscles he'd never been so aware of. Finally, Zed felt Flick's balls against his ass and he let out a shuddering sigh.

"You good?" Flick brushed a finger against Zed's cheek.

"Not sure." The burn was still there, the stretch, but it was eclipsed by an intense feeling of fullness that Zed couldn't decide if he liked or not. It was definitely the weirdest feeling he'd ever experienced.

Then Flick rocked his hips back and forward, and Zed understood why anal sex was a thing.

"Oh my God," he breathed. "Again."

Words abandoned him shortly after, leaving him awash in sensations. That magic spot Flick had teased earlier—his prostate—sparked incessantly now, stimulated to the point of mindless, almost-but-not-quite pain. Zed's mouth dropped open and his head fell back, totally incapable of rational thought, or words, or even making sounds.

It was so goddamned *good.*

Flick shifted position and he was suddenly pegging Zed's gland on every thrust. Zed's eyes rolled back and his hands struggled to find something, anything, to hold onto. He settled for Flick's arms, grabbing them right above the clenched fists that belied the intensity of it all for Flick, too.

"Getting close," Flick gasped. "Fuck...oh, fuck."

Oh...that was something else he could grab. One of his hands flailed for his dick. He gave it a stroke, thinking he could come from just that one caress—but his body was so overstimulated, it was almost painful. He'd have to chase his orgasm, and he did, timing his strokes to Flick's thrusts. Sounds started to emerge from his throat, whimpers he might have been embarrassed about if it was anyone but Flick hearing them.

But it was Flick. The man he loved.

Flick's hips snapped forward, and he let out a strangled yell, his hands shifting from the bed to hold Zed's hips, the fingertips digging in hard. Flick was coming—coming inside of him—

And that was enough to send Zed over the edge too. A hoarse shout ripped from his throat. It might have been Flick's name, might have been a curse, might have been nothing at all but an animalistic sound of release. His cock jerked, semen fountaining over his abs, as Flick continued to pulse inside of him.

Best fucking feeling ever.

"Jesus," Flick rasped, falling forward. "Jesus."

Zed let his hands fall to his sides, even as his body gave another jerk, another spasm. He felt utterly boneless, incapable of moving. His eyes slipped to half-mast and he knew his lips were slightly curved—but he didn't fucking care.

Slowly, Flick pulled back, separating them, and even the sensation of his come trickling from secret places couldn't rouse Zed from his stupor. A chuckle floated over him and the mattress shifted as Flick flopped beside him.

"In the dictionary beside 'well-fucked' is a picture of you," Flick said, the pride in his contribution to Zed's state apparent. "You okay?"

Zed opened his mouth, but his tongue and throat didn't really want to work together to make any sort of intelligible noise. He settled for a grunt and nod instead.

"I've fucked the ability to talk out of you. I'm awesome." Flick chuckled. "When my legs work again, I'll get a towel to clean us up." He rested his head on Zed's shoulder. "Guess we don't have to worry if we're sexually compatible."

Chuckling, Zed tilted his head to press a sloppy kiss to Flick's temple. Nope, definitely not something to worry about.

It was tempting to lie there until they fell asleep—the fact they'd not long been awake notwithstanding. Over the past couple of years, Felix had rarely had the luxury of lying beside a lover, wrapped in the warmth of the afterglow. He wanted to bask in it. He wanted to count the ways he loved Zed—maybe out loud. He wanted to cuddle and talk and nuzzle and just be.

It was weird, but familiar in a way he couldn't describe.

It felt *right*.

Zed's heart beat slowed with his breath and Felix wondered if he'd slipped under the same spell. Maybe he'd just fallen back asleep. Then Zed's hand found his, fingers threading through Felix's fingers. He squeezed gently and the touch said more than words ever could.

Felix remembered the first time they'd held hands. It hadn't seemed to mean much. Zed was stuck in a duct—he'd been chasing Felix through the bowels of Pontus Station. Felix had nicked his wallet, so the chase was fair game until Zed tried to shove his well-fed body through the same tight air duct Felix so often used to lose pursuers. Felix looked back, ready to thumb his nose at the other boy, and stopped. Zed's expression had not been one of defeat, anger or even humiliation. Instead, he'd smiled, clearly acknowledging Felix's win.

Felix wouldn't have trusted that smile on any other face. He couldn't even say why he had then. But he climbed back into the duct and offered Zed his hand. They grasped wrists, just as the heroes did in the adventure holos, and Felix had pulled him out. Zed let him keep the wallet and they'd been friends ever since.

The second time they held hands hadn't seemed as important until now. It had been their first day at Shepard Academy and Felix had been scared witless. He'd been the smallest, the most poorly dressed, the student with the least amount of luggage. He had an accent, a truncated way of speaking developed by generations of station born, and no formal education. He didn't belong. He'd been staring up at the imposing buildings of the academy, ready to bolt, when Zed caught his hand and entwined their fingers, much as he'd just done. He squeezed and smiled that smile of his, the one that always made Felix feel as if he was the only other person in the galaxy.

"This is just the beginning, Flick."

"No such thing as endings and beginnings. Only middles."

He'd hoped to sound smart and brave.

Now, ten years later, Zed said, "We must be in the middle by now."

Felix laughed—struck by how Zed had known just what he was thinking and glad their thoughts had returned to the same day. Thinking forward had never been Felix's thing—because the present moment was the one they all lived in, right? Same was true back then, same was true now.

He squeezed Zed's hand in return. This time, he had nothing to prove. Oh, he was scared witless, still, but felt no need to cover for it. It was what it was. "Definitely in the middle," he said, lifting his chin to invite another kiss.

KISS THE GUARDIAN

The crew of the *Chaos* spend time at the carnival on Wenchang Station.

"Kiss the Guardian" is set between *Chaos Station* and *Lonely Shore* and was written for a flash fiction event.

Wenchang Station, 2269

It was just an average delivery job until the clown rolled by on a unicycle.

For a second, Zed thought he'd hallucinated it. Alien poison was flowing through his veins, after all, and God knew what form his mental degeneration would eventually take. Hallucinations were a definite possibility. He'd never had a particular *thing* for clowns—good or bad—but hallucinations didn't care, right?

He breathed a sigh of relief when Flick muttered, "What the *fuck*."

"I...do not know." Qek clicked, her broad, blue face smoothing as she tried to understand what had just moved past them. "That...I have never seen such a thing before."

"Oh my God, is the carnival *today*?" Ness grabbed Elias's arm, as if she were trying to stop herself from bouncing. Her wild red curls vibrated with the aborted movement as the captain looked at her with an expression stuck somewhere between amusement and confusion. "We've got to check it out."

Flick narrowed his eyes. "Wait, what carnival?"

"*The* carnival." Ness waited for them to clue in, but even Zed was drawing a blank. "You guys seriously need to absorb some culture at some point," she said on a huff. "Wenchang Carnival. It's a big deal, used to happen twice a year? Ring a bell?"

That sort of did tickle a memory, actually. "Before the war, right?"

"Yeah, and this is the first one since the war ended. And we're here while it's on! I always wanted to check it out." Still holding Elias's arm with one hand, she gripped Qek's with the other. "C'mon, Captain, you're going to win Qek and I some stuffed animals."

"Oh...great." Though Elias's voice was dry, his expression had slipped fully into the amused side of things.

Zed looked at Flick. Flick looked back. He couldn't quite read his lover's expression. Were his brows lowered because he thought the carnival was stupid or because he was trying to figure out how the ship's doctor could be reduced to an excited schoolgirl by the promise of cheap toys?

"You, uh…" Zed shrugged as they trailed after the rest of the *Chaos*'s crew. "You want to check it out? I could try winning something for you."

"Or maybe *I'll* win something for you."

"I have better aim."

"I figure out angles."

"I'm stronger."

"I'm trickier."

"Are we seriously arguing about who's going to win what?"

"Maybe." Flick eyed the colorful stalls that came into view as they rounded a corner. "Want to make it interesting?"

Zed couldn't stop the smile that bloomed on his lips. He had a flash of what they'd been like back at the Academy—always up for fun and games. "What, we're competing now?"

"Whoever wins the most challenges—"

"Gets the most toys?"

Flick glared at him. "No. Whoever wins the most challenges gets to have the other person do one thing for them."

"Just one?"

"Greedy bastard. You in or out?"

Zed's grin widened. "Oh, I'm in."

Being tricky meant choosing the game that made the best use of Felix's talents, and that meant not trying Ring the Bell.

"Aww, c'mon, it's just for fun." Zed smiled his most winsome smile—or simply plucked another charmer from the collection. "And you'll like the thing you have to do for me." He winked. "Promise."

Zed was obviously thinking of sexy things. Felix liked sexy things. "Fine."

Elias went first. Felix did not laugh when the captain failed to ring the bell. Nessa gave it her best, swinging the mallet against the plate with a small shriek. She did not ring the bell. Felix didn't really care if Zed managed the feat, he simply enjoyed watching his man move—his grip on the mallet handle, the way his torso twisted, the bunch of musculature in his arms. He rang the bell.

Despite his contrary nature, Felix gave it his best shot. The holographic arrow darted up from the plate and stopped just short of the bell. The silence was deafening. Mustering a smile, he handed the mallet to Qek.

"Give it all you've got!" Nessa encouraged, jumping and clapping her hands like a toddler.

Qek's forehead smoothed, a sure sign of thought. Then she swung the mallet down with surprising force. The arrow shot up the pole and slammed into the bell.

"Damn."

"And the winner is our ashushk friend!" the barker announced, handing over a fluffy approximation of a Gentian squirrel.

Qek counted the tentacles, perhaps checking for anatomical correctness. "I have not seen a live Gentian squirrel, but in the pictures I have seen, they are not pink."

"It's a toy, Qek."

"Do adults play with toys?"

Nessa cuffed the side of Felix's head before he could instruct their pilot further in the art of human sexuality. "Hey." He rubbed his offended curls.

"Think of it as a keepsake," Nessa said.

Producing a wrinkled smile, Qek stuffed the squirrel under her arm. "What will we play next?"

Elias was scratching his head. "How come Qek managed to ring the bell harder than Zed?"

"I deduced it was a matter of applying the correct amount of force to exactly the right point of the plate."

Zed laughed. "Okay, let's see you apply science to Whac-A-Lem."

Qek whacked the Lems that were only thinking about poking their holographic noses out of their holes. Then she bowled a perfect game of Skeeball. When all of her stupidly light ping pong balls found their way into fishbowls, Felix had to bite his lips over a pout. How was she doing this? More importantly, without any points, how could he convince Zed to help him flush the water cycler aboard the *Chaos*? Sexy favors be damned, that was a messy job and he wanted help with it.

The little blue ashushk bounced up and down on her toes, a move obviously borrowed from Nessa, as she collected her prize for popping the most balloons with a dart.

Felix elbowed Zed. "You were covert ops, man. How come you can't kill six balloons with four darts?"

"Because it's not fucking possible!"

"Qek's green giraffe begs to differ."

Grumbling, Zed led the way to the shooting gallery. "Okay, this is where we'll separate the men from the ashushk."

Nessa's hand shot out before Zed could duck and he got his first cuff of the afternoon.

Felix leaned in to Zed's side. "You know Qek looks after the weapons stored aboard the *Chaos*, right? She can break down a plasma rifle in thirty-seven seconds."

Zed gaped and Felix wished he had a ping pong ball. His mouth formed the perfect O.

Qek won the match—passing off yet another stuffed animal to Felix—and then she met her match. "I do not understand the point of the next game."

Felix glanced up from an intense study of the neon yellow python wrapped around his wrist. The faux fur was incredibly soft and the eyes were sort of cute. "Huh?"

"It's a kissing booth," Nessa explained.

"How is the game played?"

"Well, it's not a game. You just pass over some credits for the chance to kiss someone really attractive." Felix glanced at the booth's occupant and frowned. "Ah, normally it's a really good looking girl or guy. I dunno what that's supposed to be."

The booth's attendant waved them over. "Want to kiss the Guardian?"

Looked like a cross between an elephant and a Berian cockroach. This was supposed to be the most technologically advanced species in the galaxy?

Zed poked a finger toward the shimmering holo. "That is *not* a Guardian."

Elias nudged Zed in the middle of the back. "You should probably kiss it to make sure."

"I wonder what the Guardians would make of this representation," Qek mused.

"I got reliable information that this is a bona fide depiction of an actual Guardian," the barker said.

"I think you've been hoodwinked," Elias replied.

Nessa tilted her head. "I don't know. I think it has a certain majesty."

Zed slung an arm around Felix's shoulders. "Well, I'm not going to kiss it. Not when I got a perfect pair of lips right beside me."

Corny as hell, but the declaration warmed Felix's middle. "Neither of us got any points," he murmured, putting his mouth close enough to Zed's for that kiss.

Zed pecked his lips. "Just as well we didn't wager with Qek."

"I would have asked for help flushing the water cycler," the little ashushk said.

"I thought it was my turn to do it?"

"Perhaps you'd like to help me with it, Fixer?"

Not really, but it would be uncharitable to say no when Qek had given him his fluffy yellow snake. Felix mustered a smile. "Okay, sure."

Zed's lips brushed his ear. "After, I can give you another job to do. One you'll enjoy."

Felix's smile spread into a grin.

"Hey, isn't anyone going to kiss the Guardian?"

Felix gestured toward Elias. "It's all yours, Cap'n. Go for it."

SALUTE TO THE SUN

For Felix, finding peace has always been about staying in motion—about running faster than his demons, and enjoying a small reprieve before they catch up. For Zed, peace is finding the center of the storm and sitting it out. Embracing stillness. Felix wants that. He's determined to learn this meditation trick. He'd like to stop running. But sitting still isn't as simple as it looks.

"Salute to the Sun" is set shortly after *Skip Trace*. I actually wrote it before we finished writing *Skip Trace*, as a Christmas gift for Jenn. In preparing to share it with our newsletter subscribers, I had to go back and edit in a few details such as nipple rings for Zed and mention their much needed therapy sessions!

I hope you enjoy this extra little episode with the guys.

Best,
Kelly

Aboard the Chaos, *2269*

Felix studied Zed's closed eyes for any hint of a twitch or half-blink. The stillness Zed managed to achieve when he meditated was unnatural. Unnerving too.

"Your eyes are supposed to be closed," Zed said, his voice low and patient.

"How do you know they aren't?"

"I can feel you looking at me."

Felix swallowed a growl. Zed's lips had barely moved and his eyelids still hadn't twitched. Bastard had some sort of super-human control. The fact that Zed was super-human, sort of, didn't make that observation any easier.

Felix had known Zander Anatolius for most of his life. Some twenty-three of his thirty-one years. There were a couple of gaps in there. Felix had apparently died, though Allied Earth Forces reports of his KIA status had been grossly exaggerated. That tended to happen when you got captured by the enemy during wartime. Zed had taken a turn at dying too. If asked, Felix would cite Zed's passing as the more traumatic event. Had damned near broken him. Might actually *have* broken him, hence his inability to sit still and pretend to meditate with his super-enhanced, alive, always larger than life lover.

Eyes still closed, Zed breathed out long and slow, as if feeding air to the atmosphere. "It takes practice, Flick." Felix's old nickname rolled off his tongue just like that, with a little flick. The corners of Felix's mouth twitched in response. "Emptying your mind is hard. Maybe start by just seeing what's in there."

What's in there? Yeah, no. Not a good idea. Felix had boxes and boxes of shit packed away in his mind, and rummaging through those carefully packed crates was most definitely not his idea of a good time. That's what they were paying a therapist for…and wasn't meditation was supposed to be relaxing?

"You don't have to dig deep," Zed continued. "Just let the surface thoughts flow past without touching them. Observe, but don't engage."

"If you're observing all this shit, why aren't your eyes moving?"

"Close your eyes, then it won't matter what my eyes are doing."

Grumbling, Felix closed his eyes. "Okay, my eyes are closed."

"Now…drift."

Drift. Huh. How had Zed had his legs? Cracking his lids, Felix peeked at Zed's legs and saw he had them crossed, ankles tucked, spread knees nearly touching the ground. Zed's hands were draped over his knees, fingers all loose and floppy. Felix shut his eyes tight and sparks ringed the resulting blackness. In the dark, he made an attempt to cross his legs, grunting as he got his right tucked, hissing as the tendons and ligaments in his left shrieked in protest.

Zed made no comment. Peeking again, Felix kept an eye on Zed's lids as he continued arranging his legs. When he had achieved a half-cross, he gripped his knees and forced his eyes closed again. The sparks returned, resolving quickly to leave a murky, pixelated gray shadowed by the afterimage of Zed's silhouette and a crescent of light from the desk lamp. Never entirely comfortable with the dark—the ultimate irony considering he spent 99.99 percent of his life in space—Felix filled in the blank spaces with what he remembered of his quarters. The desk behind Zed, currently cluttered with half-finished projects and tools. The narrow shelf jutting out over the desk. The finished projects on the shelf—small mechanical toys, a holo projector with a hazy schematic overhead, a short stack of ration bars, some data chips... Hey, maybe that pressure clamp he'd been looking for was up there.

"Are your eyes open?"

Narrowing his *maybe* open eyes at Zed, Felix swallowed a sigh and began the laborious task of unfolding his legs. To say that nearly four years in a stin work camp had robbed him of flexibility would be putting it mildly—which was why he preferred to meditate while in motion. He needed to move in order to stay moving. With a glance at the heavy kick bag occupying the corner of his quarters, Felix said, "I can't do this sitting and not thinking thing. I need to move. That's why I have my kick bag and mat."

Eyes still closed, Zed offered a short nod. He appeared completely unruffled by Felix's inability to sit still, think *still*. But Felix knew that face. He knew those eyelids—fringed with gloriously long and dark lashes—almost as well as he knew the steel blue irises beneath. He'd watched Zed sleep a few times. Probably more than a hundred times. At the Academy when they'd bunked together, or just flopped together, on Hemera Station when Zed had slept the sleep of the well and truly fucked, and way too often over the past couple of months while Zed recovered from the debilitating seizures brought on when he exercised his super-self. When he tested the *gifts* the AEF had given him.

Zed was fixed...*now*. Death could do that for a man. Shake out the old, bring in the new.

Felix was not fixed, and even now, in the face of Zed's peacefulness, he could feel pieces of himself breaking away, crumbling, dissipating into clouds of dust before they hit the floor. Swallowing a lump that may or may not be dust traveling from his brain to his gut, Felix backed away from Zed's aura, stepping outside the warm circle of peace. His agitation felt apparent. He'd already teased a thread free from a seam on his utility pants. Continuing to hang around would only poke a hole in Zed's cozy blanket of Zen.

"Don't go."

"I'll just mess with your thing if I stay."

Zed's head tipped toward the kick bag. "Work out, then."

"I'll make noise."

"You make noise when you sit still."

Felix scratched his cheek, then let his fingers crawl over his ear and into short curls. "Well, yeah, I can't sit still is why. My knees are all fucked up."

A faint smile rippled across Zed's wide and sensuous mouth. "Kick your bag, then. Get 'em all loose."

After considering his position a moment longer—weighing leaving versus staying—Felix moved to his kick bag and began a warm up. By the time he had the bag swinging away from his most powerful kicks, Zed had disappeared. His body was there, but he'd gone somewhere else mentally, to that place Felix couldn't reach. To the place the Guardians had given him, that nirvana of health and wholeness that would forever be beyond Felix's grasp.

But didn't mean he couldn't try to get there, even if he had to kick his way through a new bag every month.

If the Net could teach him how to get rid of fruit flies—they were gonna start irradiating every goddamned crate of fruit carried into their cargo hold—it could teach him how to meditate. He might not find that wholeness Zed exhibited. Felix hadn't been broken down and put back together by superior beings. But if he could touch that peace, stroke it with one mental finger, maybe he'd get an idea of what Zed did with that hour every morning. Find some of that glowy shit that flushed his cheeks with…glowy shit. Okay, he'd never look as hearty and hale as all that, but… Fuck it. Was it so wrong to want to be whole? To at least be able to imagine what that might feel like?

Every search he'd run so far detailed varyingly frustrating ways of remaining still.

Maybe he could invent his own meditation system. Some martial arts were supposed to be meditative, weren't they? Teasing his lower lip with his tongue, Felix poked at the holographic keyboard projected over his desk. *Martial art meditation.* Oddly, a blush crept out of his shirt collar, up his neck and over his ears. It would be less weird to search for ashushk porn, right?

His search resulted in a series of images, each depicting a figure sitting cross-legged. What the fuck was it about being able to cross your legs? That was some painful shit. If—*if*—he could get his knees all folded like that, and pointed somewhere toward the floor, then his hips ached. And his back. After a minute, his shoulders got into the act. He'd lasted three minutes yesterday.

Zed had been all patient and encouraging. Told him that if he divorced his mind from his body, the pain would fade. Only way Felix knew how to free his mind was with sex. Or movement. Glancing sideways, he regarded his kick bag. The heavy SFT material was starting to show its age, dead patches of smart fiber covered by stains. Sweat, blood. Some tears. Mostly sweat.

Felix turned back to his console and reached up to poke through the collection of articles his search turned up. Nope, nope, nope... huh, what was that? Yoga. Sounded like an ice-cream flavor. With a flick of his fingertips, he expanded the article. Oh, yeah, crossed legs, nope, wasn't going to work. Hey, wait a minute...

He pulled a series of images to the forefront of the display and scrolled through them. A figure standing, reaching tall, then bending down. Doing a runner's stretch, a push-up, sticking his ass in the air, another runner's stretch, touching his toes and standing up again. No crossed legs.

"This is it. I can do this. *This* is gonna be my thing."

The article described the sequence as a "Salute to the Sun." It was supposed to be meditative. Encouraged, Felix pushed back from his desk and, eyeing the projection, performed the series of moves. His joints creaked and his tendons grated, but he got through the sequence with little effort. What's more, he enjoyed the sense of rhythm that came with repetition of the movements, or poses as they were called. After twenty reps, his chest heaved pleasantly and sweat beaded his brow.

And, he'd thought of nothing but moving.

It was kind of like a workout with the bag, but not as grueling. He didn't have to wrap his hands and, without a visual target, his thoughts hadn't latched onto the idea he had to kill something dead. Defeat all foes.

The door to his quarters slid open and Zed stepped through the hatch, ducking his head even though he had a couple centimeters of clearance. It was a good habit for a tall man.

"What's up?"

Making an effort to calm his breathing, Felix tried for a nonchalant shrug. Just one shoulder. "Nothing much."

Stepping close, Zed ghosted a hand over his damp brow. "Been working out?"

"Meditating."

Zed's blue eyes cut sideways to the kick bag, which hung still. One dark brow quirked upward. "Oh yeah?" Zed glanced toward his groin.

Felix gave him a light shove. "Not that kind of meditation." When Zed's gaze roamed toward the open holo, Felix quickly reached back to pinch the display, crumpling the image as if it were paper.

Zed held up his hands. "Not gonna ask, but if you're looking for Qek's stash of instructional vids"—on human sexual technique, no thank you—"I can hook you up."

"I'm not looking at porn." Anger spilled into his gut. Even as it spread, Felix could tell it was unreasonable, a defensive mechanism he had little control over. But Zed had to know he was sensitive about this shit. "I just..." He didn't want to demonstrate his stupid sunny salute thing. It wasn't sitting still with an expression of blissful calm, and he really didn't need that difference pointed out while any peace he'd gained from the exercise rapidly steamed off his heated skin.

Angling his shoulder past Zed, Felix made for the door. "I gotta go clean the—"

"Hey." Zed caught his arm, pulling him to a gentle halt. "Flick, I didn't mean—"

"It's okay." It wasn't, not really. He glanced up to meet Zed's gaze and found befuddlement. Well, he was confused too. Lifting his heels, he reached up and caught Zed's full lower lip between his teeth, delivering a sharp nip. Hissed breath tickled his mouth. Releasing his prize, Felix added a dash of sugar. A quick kiss and a wink.

Then he ducked through the hatch, leaving Zed standing in his quarters, looking properly confused.

So, there was more to yoga than the one salute to the sun. There were more salutes too. Different poses, and he was supposed to breathe in a special way as he moved from one to the next. *In* as he stretched, *out* as he contracted. When he got the two confused and tried to breathe in as he contracted, weird things happened to his gut.

There were plenty of cross-legged positions—or as Felix preferred to think of them, folded-leg positions. One of the women in the holos had arranged her legs like a fucking pretzel. Seriously, they looked like a tangled spool of wire beneath her.

"And what the fuck is that?" His surfing finger paused over a man—legs broken beneath him—who had his head tipped back so he could pull a strip of fabric from his open mouth. Apparently he'd swallowed it, on purpose, to clean his insides. "Yeah, well, my soul ain't never gonna be that pure."

He'd stick with the external stuff.

Okay, these looked good. Balance postures. Mountain, tree... Fucking weird names, but... Okay.

Felix pushed away from the console and stood as directed by the instructional holo he'd queued up. Feet hip width apart, knees slightly bent, thigh muscles engaged, which meant pulled toward his hips. Stomach tucked toward his tailbone, shoulders back and down. Spine straight. Just getting himself lined up took concentration and by the time he finished, he felt nothing like a mountain. He felt more like a broken stick. Maybe he'd got tree and mountain confused?

The guy on the holo—hey, wasn't that the same guy who'd just pulled cloth out of his throat? Felix bent forward to peer at the small pixelated face, then enlarged it. Man, that was a peaceful face. Too fucking peaceful. The guy looked as if... Hell, he looked as if he'd just come sixteen times. Shouldn't even be standing, let alone trying to look like a mountain. Oh, right, hands over his head.

Felix put his hands up, palms together in prayer position. At least no one had asked him to actually pray. In fact, the whole yoga thing seemed less focused on communing with an actual god as with himself.

Probably not the best instruction for a former prisoner of war.

Losing his focus, Felix tipped to the side. He fetched up against his kick bag, hugging his arms around the solid weight until he found his feet. He'd just fallen over while standing up.

"I am fucking pathetic."

And he didn't feel all that peaceful, either.

He needed something easier than standing. What about... Oh, corpse pose. Now if that title wasn't *apt*. Though, in his experience, corpses usually weren't so neatly arranged and peaceful. Nevertheless, he laid down, flat on his back, feet turned out, hands slack at his sides, and activated the guided meditation.

"Tighten your fists, hold for a breath, and loosen."

Repeat without the rinse.

The tightening and loosening thing moved from limb to limb until he was apparently relaxed. Then the voice guided him down a set of stairs that never seemed to end.

When Felix finally opened his eyes they were a little crusty... and Qek was looking down at him. "Are you well, Fixer?"

Felix yawned and stretched. "Yeah. I guess I fell asleep."

"On the floor?"

"Apparently." Wriggling his fingers and toes, Felix tested his *wholeness*. Felt like he'd slept on a cold, hard floor. It'd been a good nap, though.

"No fucking way."

If he couldn't cross his legs, nothing short of a dislocated hip would place his ankle behind his head. Felix glanced down at his legs, which he had managed to loosely cross after a week and a half of practice, and tried to envisage lifting one of them up and over his shoulder. His back screeched in protest.

"Jesus, Joseph and Mary, I haven't even moved yet!" he scolded his recalcitrant body.

"Fixer to the bridge."

Thumbing his bracelet, Felix answered the captain's summons. "I'm trying to meditate down here."

"Yeah, yeah," Elias answered. *"Wash your hands before you come up, eh?"*

"Fuck you."

Why did everyone think his idea of meditation was masturbating? His pants had been securely fastened when Qek found him passed out on the floor.

"Right, we're gonna do this."

It'd been three weeks. He was getting limber. Sort of. He could sit cross-legged for eight minutes now and he'd mastered the floor nap. Corpse pose rocked.

Felix lifted his leg, grasped his ankle and tugged it toward his head. If asked, he'd have no clear explanation for why he had to put his foot behind his head. It would hurt, he already knew that. Was one of those givens, like the fact his bones ached when he got too cold. Ever since seeing it, though, the posture had teased him—challenged him. He'd spent years pushing himself toward limits, passing them and redefining them.

He'd survived four years as a prisoner of the stin. Three and a half of them deep in the mines of Isroth.

He could put his foot behind his head.

His hamstring tanged, then settled. The bones in his ankle creaked. Fire licked along one side of his back, a warning he'd stretched just a bit too far… and then he had his foot in front of his face and it was an ugly mother. He really needed to borrow one of Zed's scrubby things. The textured puff he used to loosen dead skin. According to Zed, sloughing away dead skin was good for the complexion. His wrinkled heels could use a lot of sloughing.

The moment's reflection had been enough for his thigh to stop complaining. Drawing in a breath, Felix breathed out and *contracted.* Folded his belly, dipped his head and wedged his right ankle behind his neck.

"Holy shit."

He had a single moment to revel in his accomplishment before the pain hit.

A howl tore from his throat, a primal sound that echoed from the metal walls of his quarters. When it met his ears again, his yell sounded like a scream. Felix pushed at his leg and more pain burned from the back of his knee to his groin. Letting his hands fall away, he grappled with breath—stifling another scream—and sought the place of calm he knew he'd need to get his fucking ankle off the back of his neck.

"Fuck, fuck, fuck, fuck…"

Breathe in, breath out. In, out. Tighten and release? No, fuck no…ow, ow, ow.

"Shit, shit, shit…"

He needed to calm down, which would be easier done without his foot wedged behind his head.

"Of all the stupid things."

Either the pain had begun to fade, or he'd killed his leg. Maybe shock was descending. Oh, man. If he passed out like this, the crew would piss themselves.

They'd think he'd been trying to suck his own cock, wouldn't they?

"Fuck. Okay, I need to calm down. Calm. Caaaaaalm."

Ow, ow, ow.

He needed to find that place of peace and wholeness that he'd been searching for. He needed to relax. Closing his eyes, Felix practiced a couple of the breathing techniques he'd learned. He distracted himself by trying to remember whether he'd inhaled or exhaled through his left nostril last. When he felt calm—in a fucking relative way—he tried to pull his foot away from his neck. His sweaty fingers slipped on his ankle bone. The tension in his leg remained on lockdown.

He was stuck.

"Shit."

Breathe in through the left nostril and out through the right. If he could pull the hemispheres of his brain into balance—

Ow, goddamn ow. Shit! "Double shit."

He needed to call someone. Either that, or spend the rest of his life folded in half and in agony. Who should he call?

Elias would laugh until he choked. Qek might not have the strength to help him pull his leg back over his head. She would also likely make several embarrassing observations while making the attempt. Zed... Zed would collapse onto the deck with Elias, hooting and howling.

He'd have to call Nessa. This qualified as a medical emergency, didn't it? And, as ship's doctor, she'd have to keep his confidence. He couldn't count on her not to pass judgment, but he could count on her not to tease him...verbally. She'd laugh with her eyes instead.

Releasing his hold on his ankle, Felix tapped his bracelet. "Ness."

"*What's up?*"

"I, um... I need some assistance in my quarters."

"*You all right? You sound kind of breathless.*" Her concern was evident through the comm, as well as her unasked questions. Had he discovered where she'd hidden the sedatives? Had he found some other supply?

"I was..." *Don't say meditating.* "Exercising and... got stuck."

After a beat of silence, she answered, "*On my way.*"

She tried not to laugh, he could see that. To her credit, the surprise in Nessa's expression far outweighed any humor, but once she got over the shock of finding her ship's engineer with his ankle wedged behind his neck, mirth lit her merry brown eyes.

"What were you doing?"

"Not jerking off." Or trying any other method of self-pleasure.

"I can see that." Her features took on a business-like cast while she ran her hands up and down his thigh, the touch not intimate but stupidly embarrassing. "Lord, Fix, the muscle here is so tight. How did you even get your leg back like this?"

"Determination."

She bit her lips together, cheeks rounding to either side. "But why?"

Huffing out a breath, Felix related a version of his story. His search for a meditative technique, his discovery of yoga.

"This is yoga?"

Felix waved at the holo display where the dude with the broken legs continued to look completely blissful. He's obviously dislocated his brain from his body somehow.

"That does not look like fun." She pressed her thumbs into the back of his knee. "Okay, you need to relax or we'll never get your leg down."

"Then stop asking me why I put it there."

Of course the hatch to his quarters slid open right then to reveal Zed, who paused in the act of ducking to stare, openmouthed, at the tableau before him. "What the ever loving fuck."

Elias's face poked out from behind Zed's bulky shoulder. "Holy crap."

Behind the pair of them, Qek clicked.

Kill me now.

Leaving off her ministrations, Nessa stood to shoo away their audience. "What are you all doing here?"

"You ran down to engineering waving your medical wallet," Elias said. "What do you think we're doing here? I thought Fix must have got his hand stuck in the core or something."

"Thanks for the vote of confidence, Eli." Shouting had the effect of tightening the tendon along the back of his leg. Fuck. He had to remember that.

Recovering his composure, Zed stepped inside. "Can I help?"

"Actually, yes. We need to relax the muscle in his leg so that we can get his foot out from behind his head."

"How did—"

"I wasn't jerking off." *Must. Not. Shout.*

"Perhaps a muscle relaxant would be in order?" Qek said.

Nessa nodded at Qek. "I might have to."

"Aww, Ness, those always mess with my stomach." Muscle relaxers and Felix were old foes. He'd broken so many bones and torn so many muscles that his body often felt like a worn out kick bag. Some mornings, his back spasmed and his neck locked up. Regular work outs usually kept him limber, but putting his leg behind his head had probably reversed two years of progress.

"It's either that or we wait for you to calm down."

With all the crew in his room looking at him like he'd sprouted a second head.

"Hit me."

She fiddled with the dial on her medical wallet. The hypo hissed and seconds later, his body melted into a pile of goo, limb by fucking limb. Zed and Ness eased his ankle out from behind his head. Elias fetched a bucket. Qek held his head while he vomited.

Nothin' like crew.

Curiously, their care did not smother him. Not completely. And in it, he found a measure of peace, but not the sort he'd been looking for.

He woke up with Zed's nose pressed to his cheek.

"What are you doing?"

"Smelling you."

Felix shifted and turned his head so that he could press his nose to Zed's. "That's weird."

"Tell me you've never smelled my skin."

After a pause in which Felix could not deny he'd ever inhaled the scent of his lover, deeply and profoundly, storing the essence of him against every future, Zed smiled—the movement of his lips only visible as a bunching of his cheeks and wrinkling around his eyes.

"Ass."

Zed pressed a kiss to his mouth. "Takes one to know one."

With a grunt, Felix disengaged, pulling back far enough to bring Zed's face into focus, and put a little space between them. Breathing space. "Did I get to brush my teeth before I passed out?" Felix ran his tongue over his relatively smooth teeth to answer his own question.

"Yeah, you pretty much insisted on it."

"I've had experience waking up with my face in a puddle of puke."

"You don't say." Zed pursed his lips. "So…"

"Why did I have my leg behind my head?"

"Looked bloody painful."

A smile creaked across his face. "It was."

Zed stroked his cheek, large fingers tweaking his ear before disappearing into his hair. Closing his eyes, Felix leaned into the caress. He could meditate like this. With Zed touching him, caring for him, he could find the will to let go. And he didn't have to go far, he could just slip into the man next to him, claim his skin, *his* peace, wear it as his own for a while.

Felix opened his eyes. "I was trying to meditate." Zed's eyes widened. "It's called yoga."

"But you don't even like sitting cross-legged."

"I still don't. I'm getting better at it, but—"

"You've been practicing sitting with your legs crossed?"

Felix shrugged the shoulder he had pressed into the bedding. "I thought if…" A sigh gusted out of him and suddenly looking at Zed became too painful. He closed his eyes again, hoping the act of shutting them would dampen the urge to tell Zed he wanted to be like *him*. That he craved his health and wholeness.

Zed continued rubbing his head, fingers sifting through short curls as they navigated the curve of his skull. "So sitting still isn't your thing."

"You think?"

"Nor is putting your leg behind your head."

"You look so fucking peaceful when you meditate. It's... kinda scary." Opening his eyes, Felix discovered a Zed who appeared more concerned than peaceful. "I don't know if I could do that. Go to that place. I think if I ran out of things to fight, I'd—"

What the fuck was he saying? He really should be saving this for their therapist.

Zed curled a hand around his shoulder and pulled him into a hug. Craving the warmth and comfort of his lover's embrace, Felix melted against him, tucking a knee between Zed's and putting a hand around his hip. He breathed in the scent of Zed— woodsy soap and heated skin, that hint of sex which was probably just Zed being Zed.

"Your thing is movement, Flick." Zed's chest rumbled beneath the words. "It always has been. You're still enough when you tinker, but it's when you move that you're most at peace."

"Feels wrong."

Zed's lips claimed his ear, nipping along the ridge. "Not wrong." His breath washed over the fine hairs at the back of Felix's neck, stirring and arousing.

Could movement equal peace? Could he be chasing a ghost?

Flattening his palm to Zed's chest, Felix pushed, encouraging Zed to lie on his back. He climbed aboard to straddle Zed's hips. They were half-dressed—shorts, no shirts—and he vaguely remembered Zed helping him to the bathroom and back, stripping off his clothes and all but carrying him to bed. Felix's muscles had been too relaxed for him to do any of it himself.

"You could have taken advantage of me last night," he said.

Zed showed him a lazy smile. "As if I need to wait for you to be drugged."

"You could have topped."

In the same tone, Zed said, "Like I care who tops or bottoms. So long as it's you."

Felix leaned forward, smoothing his hands up over Zed's chest, fingertips sifting through dark curls. He loved Zed's chest hair—the feel of it beneath his palms, the tickle of it against his chest or back. Zed wasn't a bear, but he was the hairiest lover Felix had ever had and he adored every single curl. He toyed with one of Zed's new nipple piercings, grinning at the slight hiss issuing from Zed's parted lips, and bent down to catch the tight little nub of flesh and metal between his teeth. The small point hardened further beneath his flicking tongue. Moving to the left, Felix delivered the same sweet torture, Zed's catching breath and light moans sending coils of arousal through his center.

Sex really was the best meditation, except…

Felix lifted his head. "I did this thing called 'Salute to the Sun' and I liked that. You start standing, then stretch a couple different ways while breathing. Maybe you'd like to do it with me sometime?"

To his credit, Zed didn't immediately moan and ask why they were talking about meditation while Felix sat on his hardening cock delivering lightning strikes to his nipple piercings via his tongue. Felix would have moaned. Hissed a bit. Maybe complained. Instead, Zed managed a warm and companionable look. A peaceful look. "Sure." Then, fastening one of his ever-warm hands around Felix's hip, he said, "I'll always be here, you know that. Whatever you need. You want to talk, we'll talk. You want to move, we'll move."

Felix arched a brow. "And if I want to fuck?"

Zed grinned in response.

Felix felt it then, the peace that usually eluded him. Stillness, movement, therapy, meditation... It would all be meaningless if he didn't have Zed. Then there was this, the thing they could do together, and only together, without conscious effort. Because it was natural. Because it was... *theirs.*

Leaning forward again, Felix traced the tip of his tongue up the side of Zed's neck. Nipped the stubbled line of his jaw. Let his fingers roam over every line of beloved musculature that cut Zed's torso into perfection. Kissed his shoulders, sucked on the lobe of each ear. He worshipped his lover and his friend, the man who meant everything to him. The man who had died and come back—who had broken him, and wanted to help rebuild him.

He tended the center of his own personal galaxy, making Zed writhe beneath him. His heart, his fragile heart that had to beat outside his body, in the soul of another.

God, he loved this man. Words always failed him when he tried to express how he felt. But he could do this, he had this.

And this was his peace.

"You are my sun," he said, lips coasting down Zed's cheek.

Zed breathed in. His eyes shone.

With his mouth, his hands, his body and his soul, Felix gave salute to his sun.

HONEYMOON

Zander Anatolius and Felix Ingesson are two of the hardest working men in the galaxy. They really need a break. So, we've sent them on a honeymoon—and managed to do so without bringing them to further harm.

(If you've read all five books of the Chaos Station series, you're likely breathing a huge sigh of relief here, as you're more used to people dying. Or at the very least losing limbs. This holiday has been a long time coming.)

We didn't just write this story for the Zed and Felix, though. We wrote it for the readers, the fans who have followed the adventures of Zed and Felix from the very start. For those who have mourned their losses, and cheered their successes. For all the folks who sent us little messages saying: "I cannot believe you did that!" Or: "Hasn't Zed been through enough?" Or, popularly: "OMG, Felix!"

Jenn and I also wrote this one for ourselves. We'd said goodbye to Zed and Felix with the last edit round of *Phase Shift* (Chaos Station #5), and it was hard to let go. Many of our blog posts for the release of *Phase Shift* reflected on how hard it was to say goodbye to characters we'd given life to through five novels and a small collection of short stories. So "Honeymoon" is our last hurrah—a chance for us to just play with the guys, our dear fictional friends; to enjoy their love and everlasting happiness; to share their last adventure with our readers.

We hope you enjoy this last journey with Zed and Felix.

Best,
Kelly & Jenn

Chapter One

Aboard the drift cruiser Biswas, *2270*

"Bingo!" the old blue-haired lady beside Zed chirped, thrusting her hand over her head to get the caller's attention. "Ha! Eat it, sucker!"

That last bit was directed at Zed, and it was so unnecessary. He'd never wanted this bingo excursion to turn into some sort of competition, but the lady had somehow decided they should be archrivals or something. Just because he'd won every game so far...

It wasn't like he was going to keep the money—he sure as hell didn't need it, and this was all for fun. He was going to donate the winnings to charity. Sharing that with his seat-mate didn't endear him, though—if anything, she'd gotten more belligerent at the news.

Whatever. He'd had enough. Maybe Flick was done napping and they could find some real fun. He pushed away from the table. "Thanks for the games, ladies."

There were a few murmurs from the other ladies, but his archrival shot him a glare. "That's right. You run away now. Buh-bye." Then, under her breath, "Sucker."

Zed barely managed to refrain from rolling his eyes as he left the bingo hall and started back toward the suite aboard the pleasure cruiser *Biswas* that he was sharing with Flick. His husband.

It was still hard to believe, that after all their history and everything they'd been through—particularly over the past year—they'd actually managed to walk down the aisle and say their vows without some galactic emergency looming over them. Everything was quiet, though Zed didn't dare make that observation out loud for fear of tempting fate, and for what seemed like the first time since their reunion, he and Flick had a chance to just…breathe. And be husbands. Before leaving Alpha Station on their drift cruise, they spent the first two days of their honeymoon wrapped up in each other in bed. Or in the shower. Or on the floor. Or the couch. And there'd been that one time hard up against the wall…

It was *awesome*.

The drift ship *Biswas* was an enormous hulk of human engineering, but Zed kind of liked the size. He didn't mind that they had to walk for fifteen minutes and traverse about three decks, at least, to get to any of the activities on board. Being off the beaten path was great—it meant their cabin was quiet, and he could almost pretend they were spending time planetside somewhere. A drift cruise hadn't been his first choice for their honeymoon, but Zed didn't think he'd get Flick down to the surface of a planet again for a long time, not after their last trip like that had ended in a crash landing and being stranded.

He was cool with compromise, though. That's what marriage was all about, right?

The door flashed green as he approached, recognizing the ID stored in his wallet, but it didn't open until Zed pressed his hand against the doorjamb and it read the lines on his palm. He stepped inside, quietly, in case Flick was still asleep.

Turned out, he needn't have worried.

Zed froze on the threshold of the suite's living room, the smile curving his lips dropping away as he took in the…carnage. That was really the only word to describe what he was seeing. He couldn't even make sense of it—all the dismembered bits and pieces scattered around the room in a horrible, graphic puzzle. With Flick sitting in the middle of it all.

"What did you do?" Zed gasped.

"Huh?" Flick looked up at him, his eyes still with that distance that said he'd been truly absorbed in a task. "I've never seen one of these before. It's a 'factor—kind of. Like that little one I made for Elias, to make 3D maps?" Zed vaguely remembered something like that—it had been a gift for the captain of their ship, the *Chaos*. "Except, it makes even bigger, more complex things. And super high quality. Look!" Flick held up a silk shirt in the vibrant cool colors that Zed preferred. It had the sheen of expensive smart-fiber tech, rather than the dullness Flick's shirts usually sported after a couple of days. Flick was *hard* on clothing.

But...no, that sheen wasn't just from the quality SFT. "Are those crystals?"

"Yeah! Isn't it cool? There was a huge selection of customizations available, more than I'd seen with other 'factors."

"So you took it apart."

"I had to." Flick beamed at him and...damn, it was really hard to be exasperated or annoyed when he looked so goddamned pleased with himself.

Zed eyed the mounds of indistinguishable crap strewn around Flick's legs. "Are you going to be able to put it back together?"

Flick made a dismissive noise. "Yes. Of course."

"Flick..."

"Probably," he amended. "At least I made you a shirt first, right?"

Putting the 'factor back together was neither the challenge, nor the point. Now that he'd seen the inner workings, Felix could improve it. Would improve it. The difference between any small matter printer was in the memory and extrusion models—what it could make, in how many different forms. The larger the apparatus, the more variety, therefore smaller 'factors tended toward specialization.

The giftfactor was the most complicated small printer Felix had ever seen. Designed to manufacture souvenirs and tokens, it pushed the limits of what was possible with a limited extrusion models. Now he knew why—and with parts from the neighboring snackfactor, his refurbished model would be able to make clothing, flags, souvenir towels, crystal solar system models, sparkly retro postcards and donuts.

It would also brew coffee.

Felix tightened the last screw, flipped open the control panel and connected it to the holo hovering over his bracelet. His upgrades required a few programming tweaks. Qek's input would have been invaluable here. As he waited for the interface to update, he indulged in a moment of... Could you be homesick for a person?

Qek would be delighted by such a concept. Nessa would find it wonderfully mushy. Elias would tease him mercilessly—which was why he didn't miss Elias at all. Nope. Not one little bit. Besides, why would he miss his crew and his ship when he had everything he'd ever wanted right here. Speaking of which…where was Zed?

His neck crackled like snack nuts when he looked up from the display. Also, he couldn't feel his legs. What he wouldn't give for a good work bench. Ah, there was Zed. On the bed. Asleep. The sonorous buzz Felix had mistaken for the 'factor coming to life was in fact Zed snoring.

Not trusting his legs to work until blood flow had been restored, Felix crawled across the floor of the suite, wincing as something dug into one of his knees. A screw. He tossed it into his new pile of spare parts and continued across the floor until he got to the bed. There he tried a reverse slither, up instead of down, and succeeded in pulling most of the quilt off the side before he got onto the bed. Zed laid supine, face pointing toward the ceiling, arms and legs perfectly aligned—as if he'd only meant to lie there for a second and then drifted off.

His new shirt was amazing. Bright but not too garish—besides, if anyone could pull off color, it was Zed—and perfectly tailored to his build. He looked sexy in the shirt. Of course, Zed could work a webbed cargo restraint or a trash chute liner. He also redefined the word sexy. Made it something fuller, deeper, more meaningful.

Felix could look at him and get hard. Instantly. Hell, he didn't even have to look at Zed to get hard. A lingering whiff of his cologne could do that. Or a stray thought. The memory of what they'd been up to that morning. Zed in the shower—and how even water needed to caress his skin, defining every ripple of muscle and strong curve. The color of his eyes when he smiled, when he laughed, when he said *I love you* (or thought it). When he came.

More often than not, however, when Felix looked at Zed, he didn't immediately think with his cock. His heart took over the show—beating more furiously for a handful of seconds before falling back into a strong rhythm designed to keep him apace with Zed's love.

Zed awoke with a forehead wrinkle, a snuffle and flickering eyelids. He rolled his head toward Felix, who hadn't gotten much beyond kneeling on the side of the bed.

"Have I told you how creepy it is when you watch me sleep?" he said.

"Nope. Because you love it. Admit it—if you woke up and I wasn't there staring at you, you'd wonder where I was."

"I'd just assume you were off making trouble somewhere."

Felix huffed softly. "Shirt looks good. How does it feel?"

Zed shifted his shoulders a little. "Not the best choice for sleeping. I think the crystals have pressed a new constellation into the back of my shoulders."

"Better take it off then."

Grinning, Felix reached for the shirt buttons. Zed captured his fingers and brought them to his lips. "You just want me to take my shirt off."

"Well, yeah. I could offer you back rub or something. But really, I just want to have sex."

Or he could give a whole speech about how he felt bad for getting lost in another project while they were on their honeymoon, but Zed already knew that. He could feel it through the connection between Felix's crystal arm and the small chip of resonance in the back of his neck. The quiet loop of feedback formed an undercurrent to most of their conversations.

"You're so romantic," Zed murmured. He kissed Felix's fingertips and an extra layer of *love* zinged across their connection.

"So, about the giftfactor..." In other words: *I'm sorry I got lost in a project and then forgot to notice how sexy you looked in the shirt I made for you and then let you fall asleep while I cleaned up my mess. And I love you. Always and forever. And I can't promise never to do this again. Do you still love me?*

"I married Felix Ingesson, didn't I?"

"For some strange reason." Felix extracted his fingers from Zed's hold and went back to pulling open buttons. Zed grabbed his fingers again. "Much as I want to get naked with you right now, we don't have time."

"We don't?"

"We have about ten minutes to get ready for our spa appointment."

"Spa appointment?"

"We talked about it yesterday."

All Felix remembered about yesterday was wondering if he could combine all the 'factors in their room into one monster machine. And the sex they'd had in the shower. "Does getting ready involve having a shower?"

"Probably a good idea. It's only polite to get clean before most spa treatments."

Felix could feel his eyes narrowing. "What sort of treatments are we getting?" He vaguely recalled the conversation now. Something about blackheads (apparently his pores weren't meant to look like this) and hot stones (to melt stress away from points of tension—which actually sounded pretty good).

Mostly, he remembered Zed's desire to share something he enjoyed with the man he loved.

"Bisilius mineral wraps followed by an energy scrub and Swedish massage," Zed said.

"What does all that mean?"

Zed's grin had a slightly evil cast to it. "You'll see."

Chapter Two

Bisilius minerals looked a lot like mud and the tiny little woman with the great big smile wanted to smear it all over his naked self.

"And then we'll wrap you in pompao leaves to seal it in," she said as she continued stirring her cauldron of brown slop.

Felix glanced up from the mesmerizing turn of the flattened spoon thing. "You want to wrap me in mud and leaves like…like droppings left on the forest floor."

"Droppings?" Zed's lips twitched.

"I was trying to be polite."

"Mmm-hmm."

"We do actually offer a Kontaran faeces wrap." The little woman smiled a little wider and it was scary. She had way too many teeth and her lips were all kinds of stretchy. Who had a mouth like that? Also, people actually paid to be wrapped in shit?

Felix touched the back of Zed's hand. Before he could even form a mental word to go along with the combination of uncertainty and mild disgust whirling through his head, reassurance flooded down the line from Zed. And a hint of a plea. Zed wanted to do this. Together. Hold hands while someone smeared mud over their bodies and wrapped them up like a filthy cigar. Apparently it would be soothing and bonding and their skin would be extra super touchable afterwards. They'd slide together with less friction—if they didn't simply get off on touching one another.

Damn, now he was half-hard.

Scary mouth, whose name was actually Daphne, was pointing toward a set of shelving tucked into an alcove. "You can leave your clothes in there. Lie face up and I'll see you gentleman in a few minutes."

As soon as the door closed, Zed turned to him and said, "I love you."

A surprised chuckle turned Felix's scowl into something else entirely and Zed's immediate grin made it difficult for him to reclaim any expression of intensity. Pulling a sigh up from his toes, Felix gave up. "Nothing says love like being willing to let someone wrap you up in mud."

Zed's grin lasted all the way through undressing, lying side by side on the two hovering treatment tables, and arranging the plastic-y SFT towel over their manly bits. He then reached over to grab Felix's hand.

Felix left off studying the ceiling—patterned with tiny lights representing the starscape as viewed from the drift's current location—and rolled his head toward Zed. "These table things are a lot more comfortable than hover stretchers."

"I thought you might freak out when you saw them," Zed said.

"I thought I might too, but this room couldn't look any less like a medical facility if it tried."

Zed squeezed his fingers.

"How about you?" Felix asked. If anyone had a store of medical nightmares, it would be Zed.

"I'm good."

Felix grinned. "Very good."

Daphne knocked, entered and grinned scarily. "Right, let's get you gentlemen wrapped!" Her gaze landed on Felix's crystalline arm. "Is that synthetic skin?"

"No. And I think we should leave it out of the mud cocoon." While the mud probably wouldn't harm the resonance substance, the idea of having his second most sensitive appendage wrapped in something other than SFT brought about a return of the uncertainty and disgust. Speaking of appendages... "Are you going to be smearing mud all over our, er..." He gestured toward his dick.

Daphne's eyebrows jumped upward. "I can if you like, but genital skin can be quite sensitive. I don't recommend it."

Next to him, he could hear Zed laughing.

"What?" Oh, he wasn't... "You know what, forget I asked and pay no attention to Zed. He's got a filthy mind."

Daphne gave her mud another stir. "Okay, who's first?"

Zed nodded toward Felix. "Him."

"Me?"

"First on, first off."

"Me."

The mud was warm. Rather than compare the warmth to unholy substances, Felix tried to lose himself in the constellations across the ceiling. Daphne began at his feet and worked her way upward, slathering the mud over his skin with firm, no nonsense strokes. When she reached his groin, she tucked the little cloth in around his junk and continued on up over his hips. While grateful she hadn't handled him, Felix did wonder if it was too late to ask if he could use the bathroom.

"We have a product that might soften these scars if skin resurfacing isn't an option for you," she noted as she began smearing mud across his torso.

A lot of scars crisscrossed Felix's skin. With space—or the ships and stations in space—being rigorously climate controlled, the story of his imprisonment was usually hidden beneath long sleeved SFTs, which saved him a lot of pointed looks and unasked questions. That Daphne hadn't offered sympathy, or wanted to know exactly why he had so many scars, or why he hadn't had them treated, raised his opinion of her. Daphne was cool. She could smile as widely as she wanted.

He opened his mouth to tell her the scars didn't matter, then wondered if maybe that'd been Zed's purpose in bringing him here. To have his scars treated, his skin softened. He glanced over at Zed and saw the answer to that in Zed's steady steel-blue gaze. No touch required. Zed's thoughts were as loud as if he'd shouted them. Felix was Felix, no matter what shape or form he took. Scars, no scars. Weird crystal arm; tendency to be irrational and dumb.

"I'm good," Felix said.

Another attendant came in to do the wrapping. At first sight, Felix forgot his full bladder. Why hadn't Jamal been doing the mud smearing? He was hot with a capital H. Tall, broad shouldered, skin a shade darker than Elias's and happy, happy eyes. Felix grinned just looking at them. Also, the man had amazing hands. Huge, warm and...huge and warm. Being smeared with mud of dubious origin suddenly seemed a small price to pay in order to be manhandled by such beauty.

Unfortunately—or maybe fortunately—Jamal wasn't gay. Not even a little bit. He did not flirt, he did not touch teasingly. He simply wrapped Felix's muddy self up with quiet efficiency—and it was restful, relaxing and really kinda nice. Maybe spa treatments weren't the evil waste of time Felix had assumed they might be—except he really could use a bathroom.

"Is there any, er, caffeine in this mix? Or something like it?" Zed asked.

Felix would turn to look at him, but Jamal had just started wrapping his face. Yes, he had mud caked around his nostrils and eye sockets and while it wasn't the most pleasant part of the job, he had his pores to think of.

"Hmm," Daphne answered. "Not that I'm aware of. Most of our product is from the tide pools on Bisilius. Oh, there is a bean in here, though. From Gao Four. It's meant to improve circulation."

"That might be it." Zed sounded a little strained.

"Are you experiencing a burning or itching?" Daphne asked.

"No."

"You didn't list any allergies on the intake form. Is there something we might have missed?"

"No."

"Well, let me know if you're uncomfortable at any time! We can get you into the shower right away."

"Okay."

Small, tight answers. Zed was concentrating on something. Thinking hard. Oh... Oh! Caffeine! Was he thinking *not hard*?

Felix snickered.

"Shut up, Flick."

Jamal finished wrapping Zed and the attendants left the room with a reminder that they could be summoned at any time. Not only did the hover tables have embedded equipment to monitor their heart rate, but the door panel was voice activated.

"How's it hangin'?" Felix asked. The hardening mud around his mouth meant very word sounded short.

"Don't even," Zed returned.

"Jamal had amazing hands, didn't he?"

"Flick."

"Big. I really like big hands. Warm, too."

Zed answered with a low growl.

"I didn't get a look at Daphne's tits,"—he'd been too distracted by her sea monster smile—"but I did notice they hung kinda low when she was working on my shoulders. Did you get a good brush?"

Zed liked breasts.

"Can't say I noticed," he said, sounding a little breathless now.

"Was it hard to stay—"

"Seriously. You need to stop."

"Just let it pop, Zed. Your dick isn't covered in mud. Just lie there with an antenna pointed toward heaven and enjoy the free--"

"I hate you."

"Love you too."

Felix might have been content to lie there and think about Zed's interesting reaction to caffeine for the half hour they were slated to be wrapped. But his bladder had other ideas. "I need to take a leak."

"You were supposed to go before they started."

"Yeah, well, I was all distracted by the mud and stuff."

"Can't you hold it?"

"Do you think the sheet I'm lying on is medical grade SFT?"

"You did not just ask me that."

"Okay, fine, I won't piss on the treatment table, but I really need to go." Felix used his free arm to lever himself upward. Sitting, or folding oneself while wrapped up tight, proved difficult. The mud pulled at his skin and some of the broad leaves crinkled and cracked.

"You're supposed to be relaxing."

"How relaxed are you?"

Trying not to pop wood was like the exact opposite of being relaxed.

"Point taken," Zed hissed.

"If I can just get my legs on the floor…" Felix pushed himself to the side of the table and tried to swing a leg over. His whole body followed and before he knew it, he was sliding toward the floor. "Oh shit."

His table was obviously wired with a 'guest has left the surface' alarm. Either that or the floor had an impact sensor. After a brusque knock, Daphne pushed the door open and stuck her head in. "Is everything—"

"I'm fine," Felix said from the floor.

Daphne tore her gaze away from Zed's table with visible effort and bent to help Felix up off the floor. The leaves wrapped around his muck-caked self crackled as he fought his way upright, progress hampered by the fact Daphne seemed to have trouble averting her eyes from table number two. Zed had obviously lost the battle with biology, chemistry, or whatever caused his body's unique reaction to caffeine. The SFT cover over his crotch swung like a flag from his upright pole.

Curious, Felix glanced up at the ceiling. Zed's dick pointed to a spot just left of Tau Centauri. Or the Hub—the center of the galaxy as defined by the Guardians. "Ah, Zed, I think the Guardians are calling."

"I swear to God, Felix, if you don't shut up…"

"I'm sure guys pop wood all the time in here. Right?" Felix turned to wink at Daphne, who gestured toward his own crotch. Looking down Felix noted he'd left his own wrap on the floor with a couple of leaves. He was swinging in the non-existent breeze. "Well, then." At least he wasn't hard. Any more time wasted and he might embarrass himself in a different manner, however. "Bathroom?"

The lovely Jamal did not return to help them peel off the leaves or wash off the mud. Daphne assisted with the former and left them to their own devices for the later after informing them they had half an hour until their hot stone massage.

Did she mean half an hour to deflate Zed's erection?

Probably.

"C'mon, you." Felix led Zed into the massive shower room and pushed him under the waterfall cascading from ceiling to floor at one end.

"Ow, ow…" Zed cupped his hands over his dick.

"You protect precious while I get the mud out of our crevices."

Armed with soap and an intimate knowledge of Zed's anatomy, Felix washed every centimeter of skin. Zed protested the caresses at first. "Not helping." "Jesus, I think I'm harder." "Fliiiick." Then he simply gave in and started moaning. Felix helped himself to a little more soap, got to his knees and washed Zed's galaxy-indicating tent pole again. Then he sucked it—long and hard, working another soapy finger into a favorite crevice.

Zed came twice. His dick barely wilted in between.

The hot stone massage was more fun than being smeared with mud and wrapped with alien leaves. Felix's masseuse even worked on his neck and jaw a little. Two blowjobs in twenty minutes left an ache.

Chapter Three

Zed felt wonderfully relaxed and shiny as they walked back to their suite. It had been quite a while since he'd indulged in so much pampering—he'd forgotten his skin could even get so smooth. And Flick's cheeks seemed to be even more rosy than usual...though that could have been residual embarrassment.

"You left them a good tip, right?"

Zed chuckled. "I left them a very good tip. They deserved it."

"It's your fault." Flick grinned. "I think you scarred poor Daphne for life."

"Yeah, yeah." Zed rolled his eyes good-naturedly.

"No offense, but if you head back to the spa to get rebuffed-up, or...whatever," Flick said with a vague wave, "I'm not going."

Zed stopped and grabbed Flick's hands. Their connection snapped into place, like a metaphysical hug. "Promise you'll go with me once a year."

Flick groaned. "Why?"

"Because you look really glowy right now. I think you liked it more than you want to admit."

Flick scoffed. "Dream on, Anatolius." His eyes changed focus, to something behind Zed's back, on the wall. "Oh hey. What's a fantasy suite?"

Zed turned to check out the holo ad floating on the wall. He took a step forward, knowing most ads like this were activated by proximity and focus. An image of a sultry and scantily clad woman appeared where the placeholder text had been. She seemed to look right at Zed as she sucked on her index finger. And...okay, he was only human. There was a twinge down below. But just a twinge because he wasn't *that* super human.

"Looking for something special to share with your loved one? Eager to have a solo night to blow your mind…and other things?" The woman switched to a slender, shirtless man wearing a dog collar, eyeliner, and gloss on his plump lips. "Every fantasy you could dream of is at your fingertips in our Xanadu Suites. Customize your night of magic to fulfill all of your sexual dreams and desires."

The picture switched to a scene aboard some kind of old-time sailing ship, featuring men and women showing a lot of skin. "See how hot the deep blue sea actually is."

Another switch, this time to a scarf-laden tent strewn with pillows. "Enjoy a night of scorching passion with your harem of men and women in the endless desert." The next switch showed a picture of the suite, Zed assumed, without the holos in place. It looked kind of plain—until it transformed into a lush rainforest, complete with a loin-cloth clad hunk swinging through the trees. "Your wish is our command. Make your dreams a reality today."

"Wow," Flick said as the holo faded to black.

"That was…detailed. And very cool. But—"

A new holo popped up, a spinning question mark. "You recently viewed the ad for Xanadu Suites. Additional information has been sent to your wallet. Do you have any questions about our services?"

"No, we're good." Flick tugged on Zed's arm and they stepped away from the wall. The question mark holo blinked out of view, switching back to the generic, text-only ad.

As they started down the hall in the direction of their suite again, Zed glanced at Flick. "It was kind of cool."

Flick grunted.

"The ship looked interesting."

"It could be fun, I guess." But Flick didn't sound too sure about that.

Zed was still thinking about it as they keyed open the door to their suite. He kind of wanted to test out one of the Xanadu Suites, because when would they ever have another opportunity? But he didn't have any real desire to have sex on a pirate ship or in a make-believe treehouse. Maybe he wasn't adventurous enough.

"Do you have any sexual fantasies?" he asked as he flopped onto the couch next to Flick.

"Uh..." Flick frowned. "Why? I don't want you to surprise me with one of those suites, Zed. They're weird."

"I won't. That ad got me thinking, though. About fantasies, and if I've got any, and what yours are. We've never really talked about it."

"'Cause I don't have any."

"Are you sure?"

"Plain old sex is good enough for me."

"But...it would be kind of fun to play, right?"

Flick shifted on the couch so one leg was bent and he was facing Zed. "Maybe I should be asking *you* if you have any secret fantasies."

"I don't know if they're secret, or if they're even really fantasies." Zed's ears grew warm. "Mostly, they're thoughts and I'm pretty happy for them to stay as thoughts."

"Oh?" Flick grinned his mischievous, playful grin. "You've got to tell me now."

"Remember...thoughts. Okay?" Zed took a deep breath. "Sometimes I wonder what it would be like to have your cock inside me and another one in my mouth."

"It would probably be hot. But that's definitely not happening. I don't share."

Zed lifted his hands in surrender. "And that's fine. Thoughts only."

"You've got more, right?"

"Um...yeah. Sometimes I think about fucking you in public." He couldn't quite stop the growl in his voice.

"Jesus, Zed. Really?"

"Yeah. Like, not full on in a crowd or anything, but...in a dark booth in a restaurant where someone *might* see us. Or somewhere we can see people but they can't see us."

Zed didn't need his enhanced senses to know that Flick's pupils had dilated slightly and his breathing had sped up. "Okay…that one? That one could be fun. Next time we're on Alpha Station, you could commandeer one of the Anatolius Industries offices that overlook the promenade. One of the low-level ones."

"The ones with one-way glass, looking out?" Zed had to adjust himself. "Why is that so fucking hot?"

"Because it's forbidden." Flick's eyes twinkled, and Zed didn't miss that he'd adjusted himself in his pants, too—and his hand was still resting on his cock. "What else?"

"Watching you get yourself off."

Flick pressed his palm hard against the ridge in his pants. "Yeah?"

"Yeah. I'd be sitting across the room. Or maybe…maybe tied to the bed."

"You'd want that?"

"Just my hands. And ties I could break if I needed to."

Flick nodded. "Very doable."

"Really?"

"You brought a couple of ties with you, right?"

Zed's eyes widened. "Wait…now? You want to…"

Holy shit.

"Is that one of those thoughts you want to stay a thought?"

Yes. No. Maybe? "I don't know."

Flick knee-walked over the cushions of the couch to get closer to Zed. "You've already come twice today, and I haven't once," he said, his voice low. "I really want to."

Zed's mouth went dry. Flick in seduction mode didn't happen often—it didn't have to, since they were both usually raring to go with a single look. But…damn, Flick knew what to say. How to say it, too, in a low, gravelly voice that was raspy with desire.

"I kind of love the idea of kneeling between your legs, looking down at you, and watching your cock get harder and harder—" Flick broke off. "This sounds stupid."

"No! No, it's good. Keep going."

"Are you sure? I feel like I'm in a bad holo."

"Christ, Flick, you've got me almost ready to blow by just talking to me, so no, I think you're doing it just right."

"Either that or you have really cheesy taste."

"*Flick.*"

Flick smacked his shoulder. "C'mon, bedroom. Let's see if we can make this work."

Zed owned a lot of ties. Why he'd brought them on vacation was beyond Felix, but sorting through them for one he could twist without damaging the material gave them both a chance to recirculate a little blood. Would be a pity to get Zed all fastened to the bed so they could look at each other and explode. Zed wanted a show. Also, he was going to be incapacitated. Felix had no idea why that made his cock swell every time he thought of it, but it did.

"How about this one?"

"Any of them. Just pick a couple."

"But this one's got little light receptors in it. They'll break if—"

Zed yanked the tie out of Felix's hands. "I can buy another one."

"Why do you have so many ties, anyway? We never go to things where we have to wear ties."

Zed gave him an odd look. "Do you want to go to things where we wear ties?"

"No."

The odd look flashed toward the ceiling as Zed lifted his chin and sighed.

"What?"

Zed was all composed when he looked back down. Even had a smile tugging at one side of his mouth. "You are the most frustrating man in the galaxy."

"Damn straight. Now let's tie you to the bed with a scrap of silk that cost the lives of three thousand rare worms on Bereta and the fingers of some poor little slave girl who had to sew in all those receptors by hand."

"I don't know why I haven't come already."

Snickering, Felix followed Zed up the bed as he scooted backward until he was nested into a pile of pillows against the headboard. Felix climbed astride Zed's hips and sat looking down at his lover. His H-word. Husband. Jesus, he was married. To Zed. His best friend. Zed smiled up at him and one of those timeless moments passed where they simply looked and smiled and existed. Happy. In love. In need of nothing but the presence of the other.

"Is it weird I could just sit and look at you and love you and it makes me this happy?"

Zed's smile widened. "When you put it like that, maybe?"

"Ass." Leaning forward, Felix kissed Zed's wonderfully full lips. Quickly and efficiently, pulling away before Zed could entice him into something deeper. The tease had begun. "Right, arm up."

Zed pressed his right wrist to the headboard and frowned at the smooth expanse of SFT. "What are you going to tie me to?"

"Hmm." The headboard was one of those upholstered arrangements hotels often used to preserve the wall behind the bed from head prints and chipped plaster. Even hover beds moved rhythmically when put to the test.

Abandoning his perch on Zed's lap, Felix shuffled forward on his knees and pulled at the headboard to see if he could get his fingers behind it. No go. Nothing above it or below it, either, and the mattress frame rested on moveable slides rather than legs. He'd need three ties a side to fasten Zed to the frame, and then he'd be lying flat rather than propped up.

"Maybe we could try the couch?"

"Nothing to tie you to there, either," Felix grumbled. He'd already thought of that. Pulling the tie straight between his hands, he scanned the suite for other possibilities. "We could use the shower, I suppose. That seems kind of clinical, though. I mean, who wants to stand up in a shower, tied to the head, while someone jacks off in front of him?"

Maybe Zed would?

Before Felix could blush, Zed muttered, "Yeah, no."

"We could pile up some cushions on the floor in front of the kitchenette. I could tie you to the little cupboard door handles."

Zed glanced through the open doors of the bedroom. Felix followed his gaze. Parts from his experiments still lined the counter. Even without the mess, the place didn't scream romance, though. Or fantasy. But—

"Maybe this was a bad idea." Zed sounded all discouraged.

Felix cupped Zed's cheeks and gave him another quick kiss. "I've got a plan."

Ten minutes later, he had two hooks made out of recycled 'factor parts screwed into the headboard. Felix yanked on them one more time to test the hold, then settled back onto the bed with a grin. "How's that?"

"We're going to end up paying to replace nearly everything in this suite, aren't we?"

"For the cost of one of your ties."

Chuckling, Zed settled back into his nest of pillows and stretched one of his arms toward the new hook. Felix had positioned them so that Zed could rest his wrists on them. Seemed kinder than letting his arms dangle from ties.

"Perfect," he said. Then he wrapped the tie around Zed's wrist, threaded it through the hook, wrapped it all around again and sat back. "How's that?"

Zed gave an experimental tug. "Good. Not too tight, not too loose."

Once he had Zed all tied up, Felix crawled back down the bed to kneel between Zed's spread legs. Though still dressed, Zed had a deliciously rumpled look. His hair was all mussed from the massage and his skin still glowed pink beneath his perpetual tan. The collar of his shirt was open an extra button, and Felix could smell the oils they'd used at the spa and a hint of the mud. He leaned forward to cup the soft mound of Zed's resting cock through his pants. "How're we doing here? Any life left?"

Zed raised his hips. "For you? Always."

Kneeling back, Felix pulled his own shirt over his head, tossed it aside and reached for his belt.

"Slower. Do a tease sort of thing."

A tease sort of thing? Felix's skin itched as a shiver crept across his chest. "Not sure I'm the right guy to do a strip tease."

"You can do it."

Blowing out a breath, Felix thought sexy thoughts—which meant thinking about Zed, and not getting his clothes off as quickly as possible so they could fuck. He cupped his own slightly chubby cock and squeezed, breathing out as a fold of material dug into the sensitive head. Then he eased his belt open and shimmied his hips as he plucked at the fastening tabs on his pants. You could probably cook an egg on his cheeks by the time he was done, but Zed's heavy lidded look made his embarrassment worthwhile. As did the bulge at Zed's crotch.

Felix pushed his pants down over his hips, then left them there, figuring a state of half-undress might add to the whole ambience or whatever. Then he licked his palm and gripped his erection.

Zed let out a breathy groan and tugged at his bound wrists.

Felix squeezed his cock, which pulsed against his palm. His balls were already tight and tucked. "I don't know why you look so damned good tied to the bed like that. I wouldn't have thought it was my thing," he said.

"Don't know why not. You love having your way with me."

Felix began a slow and steady stroke. He tipped his head back and groaned softly, needing to voice his pleasure at even the feel of his own hand. Also, because if he met Zed's gaze, he'd spill his load. His balls were all tingly and prickly. He smoothed his crystalline hand over his stomach, then up toward his pecs. Zed's breath caught.

Dipping his chin, Felix noted Zed's attention was split between his cock and his wandering hand. He reached up to pinch a nipple. Zed's lips parted in a quiet gasp.

"You like that, huh?" Felix rocked his hips forward into his fist in a show of fucking his hand.

"God, yes." Zed sucked in a quick breath, only to lose it in another gasp.

Felix rolled his nipple and damn if it didn't feel good—and make the situation in his balls all the more urgent. Zed tugging against his restraints only ratcheted up the tension. Knowing Zed wanted to touch him, but couldn't. Touching Zed would be against the unwritten rules too, he supposed, though the straining fabric over Zed's crotch called to him.

"How hard are you?" Felix asked.

"Really fucking hard."

Felix teased out the length of his cock in one long stroke before twisting his hand off the end in a move he liked, that Zed always properly emulated when jacking him. "As hard as this? Are your balls aching?" He tweaked his other nipple. "Wish it was you touching me."

Zed whined and yanked at his wrists. The headboard squeaked.

Felix started stroking himself toward the finish line, hips bucking as he thrust into the warm grip of his fingers. He'd tried jerking off with both hands, the human one and the resonance one. He preferred the human one. The calluses on his palm added some interesting friction, and skin was skin. He could use a little more slick, though. Where'd they put the lube?

Ah, fuck it, by the time he crawled off the bed and found it, he could be done here and he really wanted to be done. Felix wasn't one for keeping a climax waiting, especially not when it was his hand on his cock.

He spat in his hand and pulled at his cock again, quickly working back up to speed. Then he reached down to tug at his sac, pressing the cool thumb of his crystal hand between his balls. Another roll and tug, two more strokes, and he was about there, holding off now by will power alone. Slitting his eyes open, he prepared to deliver one more taunt to Zed, get him fully riled up.

He didn't have to. Zed sat panting, shaking—no, trembling. His hips jerking up and down as he sought the friction. His arms smacked against the headboard like cargo ties being tested by fast acceleration. His face, though—the naked want, the frustration. The absolute need tempered with the knowledge he was helpless.

An urgent thrill shot down Felix's spine...and that was it. He came—suddenly and sharply, his cry oddly hoarse as he shot. He pumped harder with his newly wet hand and another jet spurted across the bed. Another, and then another. It felt as if he was trying to empty himself of three or four built up orgasms. It almost hurt. It felt fucking fantastic.

Over the sound of his own harsh breaths and throaty cries, he could hear Zed groaning and the headboard squeaking. Then a sharp crack cut through their little concert. Felix looked up. Zed had pulled one arm free. The hook still dangled from his wrist, but the headboard was toast. Same for the wall behind it. In fact...Felix tilted his head.

"I think I can see our neighbors through that hole." Which meant anyone on the other side of the wall had a great view of him milking his own cock. "Shit and double shit. Put something in the hole!"

He wasn't ready for exhibitionism. Not on top of a mind blowing orgasm. Or with Zed half tethered to the wall and the cost of damages rising every second. Zed turned to shove a pillow toward the hole and a second ominous crack reverberated through the room.

"Wait!" Felix held up his sticky hand.

Too late. The headboard swung like a pendulum, the lower half disappearing behind the bed with a great thump. Shoved away from its moorings by the falling headboard, the bed rocked backward. Zed yelled once before he dropped from sight, slipping off the top end of the bed. The remaining hook held his arm up for about a second before it tore loose from the wall. A mournful wail rose from the gap Zed had dropped into, a gap widening by the nanosecond as Felix rode the untethered bed back across the room. Something crunched behind him. Felix turned, afraid of what he might see. He'd put a serious dent in the bedroom door frame, but, thankfully, the doorway was just narrow enough to stop the bed from passing through.

"Everything okay over there?"

There was a face pressed to the hole. Felix quickly covered his limp dick. "We're fine. Nothing to worry about. Just, um, working out."

"Riiight."

"You wanna plug the hole from your side, or should we?"

"I'm putting something up now. Seen enough of your exercise to last me a lifetime, buddy."

Felix got off the end of the bed, paused to pull his pants up, and went to help Zed up off the floor. Then they assessed the damage. He'd bent the 'factor parts beyond recognition to fashion his hooks. Zed's ties were ruined. The wall behind the headboard had two holes in it. One large—now blocked with a cushion—one small and also apparently blocked.

The bed looked okay, or would be once they picked up the door and hung it back in the frame.

Felix turned back to Zed who wore a slightly constipated expression. "You look like you don't know whether to laugh or cry."

"I'm thinking about doing both," Zed said, his lips twitching toward the former.

"We can't be the only guests who have trashed a room."

Shaking his head, Zed slid back down the wall to sit on the floor. "Probably not, but this is pretty epic, even for us."

Felix sat next to him. "Pfft, please. There is no hull breach, marauding aliens or evil doctors in this scenario. Also, we haven't crash landed anywhere. It's just a little hole in the wall."

"You know, I'm wondering if this is why fantasy suites exist."

Felix laughed. "Maybe." He leaned in to nuzzle Zed's neck. "Did you have fun before we trashed the place?"

Zed turned so their lips could meet in a passing kiss. "Yeah. How 'bout you."

"I did. And we're going to do it again. We'll just plan it better next time."

"Mmm-hmm."

"What do you think Brennan would say if we sent a ripcomm asking him to install hooks over the bed in our apartment before we got back?"

Zed snorted, then chuckled, then laughed.

Chapter Four

Zed insisted on breakfast out the next morning, mostly so he wouldn't have to watch the workers going in and out of the bedroom, feeling a flush rise in his cheeks every time. It had been embarrassing enough to have to report the damage to the concierge—they couldn't let it go untended, especially since it affected the nice people next door—but the sidelong looks from the two women patching the wall were more than he could take.

Luckily, the breakfast place had everything from sweet and spicy oatmeal to eggs and bacon to some sort of dish that was supposed to be a human-safe version of an ashushk specialty. In other words, not something Flick could complain about. He wasn't normally one to care much about what he ate, but if the opportunity arose and they had time for it, he liked to try new stuff.

"Sure you don't want some coffee? Perhaps some tea?"

Flick's eyes twinkled at the server's question. Unlike a lot of restaurants, this place employed actual people as wait staff rather than depending on bots. For the personal touch, Zed supposed. Though he could do without the questioning of his order.

"I'm good with juice, thank you," he said evenly, adding a smile to emphasize he was really okay with the pineapple juice sitting on the table in front of him. As the server left, Zed lowered a glare on Flick. "Don't say a word."

As always, Flick ignored him. "So a trace amount of caffeine through the skin results in a boner that won't quit until you've come twice. What does drinking a cup of coffee do?"

Zed shifted in his seat, remembering the first—and last—full cup of coffee he'd had after Project Dreamweaver. "Use your imagination."

"I think you're supposed to contact a doctor if your erection lasts for more than four hours."

"Ha ha. Eat your breakfast, Mr. Comedian." Zed scooped up the last of his eggs benedict and ate it, then laid his utensils across his plate. "What do you want to do today?"

"Let's rent one of the fantasy suites."

Zed's eyes widened. "Seriously?"

"Yeah. Seriously. I've been thinking about it a lot. I had fun last night, but it'd be even better if we don't have to worry about breaking things. And besides, when are we going to have a chance to do this again?"

"Fair point." Zed pulled out his wallet and flipped through screens until he found what he was looking for. "The Transcendent Ecstasy suite is available."

"That's the most expensive, right?"

"Might as well do it right." With the press of a finger, Zed booked it. "Finish your breakfast."

"Maybe we should take some to-go coffee with us. You know…for fun."

Zed scowled. "It's not too late to get divorced."

"Oh, don't kid yourself." Flick chuckled. "It's been too late our entire lives."

The Transcendent Ecstasy Suite was…a bit underwhelming.

Flick took a few steps past the threshold and spun, slowly, taking in the whole lot of nothing in the room. The walls were white and bare, and other than the massive and comfortable-looking bed in the center of the room, there was nothing.

Flick turned a sardonically raised eyebrow on Zed. "I think we might've gotten conned."

Zed stepped over the threshold and let the door close fully behind him. As soon as it clicked shut, the room exploded into color. Instead of standing in the middle of an institutional room, they stood in the midst of a rainforest, surrounded by a riot of flowers. Every color in the rainbow flickered around them—and some Zed couldn't identify.

"That's more like it," Flick said with a smile and a nod.

"Please approach the bed," a pleasant female voice said. It came from no single direction.

Shooting a look at Flick, Zed grabbed his husband's human hand and followed the directions. Light flared around them and a female dressed in a flowing white toga-like dress appeared. She hovered about a foot off the ground, and the perfection of her skin and the light from within gave away that she was nothing more than an artificial construct.

"Welcome to Xanadu Suites. You have selected the Transcendent Ecstasy Suite, our most luxurious and immersive experience. With our holographic and biofeedback technology, we will transform this suite into a fantasy location to help you achieve the transcendent heights of your desire."

Flick waggled his brows. "Can't wait to experience a transcendent height of my desire."

Zed shushed him as their hostess continued. "Please select a category to explore. Historical, Modern, Futuristic, Fantasy, Alien."

"Uh..." Zed shared a look with Flick. Historical might be okay. He didn't really want to have to bend and twist his brain to do futuristic or fantasy, though. And alien? With his luck, that would put a giant bug-like stin in the center of the room. "Modern."

"Good choice," Flick murmured.

"Modern," the hostess confirmed. "Please select a subcategory. Reunited After War, Stranded on a Deserted Planet..."

Zed shared a look with Flick.

"Colony Life, Station Life, Star-Crossed Lovers..."

Flick was frowning.

"Non-Specific Erotic—"

"Yep. Let's go with that one," Flick said.

"Non-Specific Erotic Fantasy," the hostess confirmed. "First option: The Club With No Name."

The hostess suddenly disappeared and the room dimmed, the forest replaced by a night-time scene. Before them was a bar that looked like it was a few dozen feet away. It couldn't be…but damn. Whoever had created this illusion had been *good*. Zed could feel the coolness of the night air and hear the soft sound of nocturnal creatures in the distance.

"The Club With No Name," began a male voice, low and gruff, "has a particular reputation." The image moved closer, slowly, and Zed could almost convince himself *he* was moving. *So weird.* "It's said that within its walls, any sort of pleasure can be found. Tame, exotic—anything is fair game." Suddenly they were inside the club, watching a man and woman gyrate on a stage, covered with only enough fabric to leave the barest bit to the imagination. "They say that this is the place to go if you want to watch—or be watched. Or…both." The dancers stopped and looked directly at him and Flick, their faces open and sultrily welcoming. The man stroked his black-leather covered cock, making it clear he was hard, and the woman slipped fingers into her red lace panties.

"Are you game?" the announcer asked.

"Please state Yes, Not My Taste, or Next Selection," their hostess said.

"Next Selection," Flick said.

"But that…" Zed pressed his palm against the ridge in his pants.

"Yeah, I know. But maybe there's something better."

"Second option: Project Creamweaver."

Zed's gaze snapped to Flick's. No…they wouldn't…

The room changed to a space field, black with tiny pricks of light. "The galaxy is dangerous and deadly," the announcer intoned in his deep and growly voice. "It takes dangerous and deadly people to keep it safe. And the most dangerous and deadly of them all belong to Project Creamweaver."

Suddenly they were in a bunk room, with four other men in various stages of undress. Most were shirtless, but wearing camo pants. One wore only tiny booty shorts, not something the military would ever issue.

"Meet the men of the Project. Dagger, the weapons specialist." The image focused on a darkly handsome man leaning against one of the bunks, his arms crossed. "Blake, the martial artist." A short blonde guy, the one wearing the booty shorts, ran through a couple of showy kicks. "Spice, demo expert." A lanky redhead winked in their direction. "And finally, Zane, the leader." A tall, broad, dark-haired man looked at them, calmly, coolly, the intricate tattoo on his left wrist just barely visible.

"Holy shit," Zed whispered.

"Their special abilities keep the galaxy safe, but no one knows what they have to do to keep up their energy."

"I'm feeling kinda low," Blake said. "I need to be fucked!" He sloughed off his shorts and stuck his ass in the air. Spice, the redhead, leaped into action, shoving his face in Blake's buttocks and proceeding to rim him like a pro, if the moans and squeals were any indication. A second later, he slid his porn-star sized cock into Blake's ass. Zed hoped there was a scene or two cut where Spice actually applied lube or more spit or *something*.

"Fuck me harder! I need more power!" Blake screamed.

"As the newest recruits to Project Creamweaver, you're about to find out just how far each and every one of these men is willing to go to stay powered up and ready for action," the announcer intoned over Blake's cries. "You'll discover just how much effort Dagger, Blake, Spice and their leader Zane put into making sure their abilities will never falter when the dangerous and deadly galaxy needs their dark and deadly powers."

"Please state Yes, Not My Taste, or Next Selection."

Zed couldn't summon words. They were just…gone, stolen from him by what he'd just witnessed. They'd turned Project Dreamweaver into a porno. It was disrespectful, awful—and he realized that if Emma and the rest of them were around, they'd be rolling on the floor laughing, unable to breathe. Assuming Emma would stop yelling about the fact that she and her fellow female comrades had been left out.

"I'm sorry, I didn't catch that. Please state Yes, Not My Taste, or Next Selection."

"That was real, right?" Flick whispered.

Zed licked his lips. "Yep."

"Thank you for your selection! Have a transcendent experience."

"What? No! Shit!" Zed flailed a hand. "Stop! Not this one!"

"The year is 2260 and the galaxy is proving even more dangerous and deadly than expected—"

There was a fizz and a pop, and the regular lights suddenly flared to full brightness. Zed turned to see Felix holding out his bracelet comm and a grim look on his face. "I had to short it out to stop it. Sorry. That's probably going to be another damage bill."

Zed wrapped Flick up in a tight hug. "So worth it."

Chapter Five

Felix's small fix shorted out every holo projector connected to the Xanadu network, including the one manning the reception desk. Several patrons in various stages of undress were harassing the stand-in, and the temporary receptionist looked something like a wilted rag.

"Maybe we should stick around," Felix said.

Zed had his wallet out, two small holo displays open. "I left a large enough tip to replace every projector, don't worry."

"We should see if Brennan's legal team can do anything about—" He couldn't even say the name. His shoulders pinched together and his scrotum prickled. His dick felt all flinchy. "It's gotta be against some kind of law."

"Already on it." Zed looked more than flinchy.

"You all right?"

"Targeting the Anatolius lawyers on whoever created that holo drama will go a long way toward making me feel better."

Felix grasped Zed's wrist briefly. Just long enough to send his love. Zed didn't answer, but he felt the corresponding surge of deep affection.

Zed continued to tap away at a display while Felix led the way clear of their latest mess. He spotted one of the *Biswas*'s many observation lounges across the concourse and pulled Zed inside. Thankfully, it was deserted. Leaving Zed to finish composing his note to Brennan, Felix went to the shielded windows.

On a less exclusive drift, he might be looking at a wall-sized viewscreen. The *Biswas* was a luxury liner. Every deck had a lounge like this, all lined with polyglass windows. Felix had been a little nervous—and skeptical—about the windows to begin with. And thankful they didn't have one in their suite. Spending the bulk of his life in space was one thing. He'd never been one to take comfort in a view of the void between the stars, however. All that emptiness left him feeling untethered.

Zed liked views. Sunsets, the night sky, horizons, starscapes, nebulae. Felix had once found him staring at a flower. A single yellow bloom. Apparently he'd been meditating. Felix stared out at the stars with the image of a yellow flower in his mind.

He sucked at meditation, but he could do the deep and broody thought thing. He'd agreed to this cruise because they needed a vacation. The past year had been...rough. A graph of crazy highs and lows that defied any sort of scale. Was his inability to relax and enjoy down time killing Zed's vacation? Were all the breakages a symptom of his very own brand of mania?

"Hey." Their connection snapped into place as Zed tucked an arm around his waist and leaned into him before turning his attention toward the view. "Anything interesting out there?"

"I was looking for a yellow flower."

"Huh?"

"Are you having fun, Zed? Are you enjoying the cruise?"

"Sure. Aren't you?"

"I don't know. Maybe?"

Something other than the comforting presence of Zed spilled through the link. Anxiety? Felt a lot like sorrow. Or maybe guilt. Felix probed and got a heavier streak of remorse.

No sorry. I'm with you, he sent.

They didn't use the mental connection to talk often. Usually, a touch was like a check in. A brief exchange of *I'm good, you're good, we're all good*. Sometimes they passed along impressions. When they were being mushy, they communicated the deep feelings words couldn't cover.

Love, love, love, Zed sent back. His thoughts were more than just words, though. They were those deep feelings—and questions.

Felix turned to slip his arms around Zed's shoulders. He bumped his nose to Zed's and brushed a light kiss across his perfect mouth. "I'm sorry I keep breaking things."

With a dimple poking his left cheek, Zed kissed him back. Lightly, sweetly. "Doesn't matter where we are, Flick. So long as we're together."

Pulling back a little, Felix lifted his chin. "You say that, but I don't know that we necessarily enjoyed being together the last few places we were."

"I disagree. Both of us being there was the only thing that kept us alive. Sane. It's what got us here, to this point. It's why we're standing on the deck of the largest drift cruiser in human history, enjoying our honeymoon." Zed's certainty surged between them. An electric spark. He believed what he was saying. "Now, if you're done brooding, let's go find something else to break."

They ended up in a sports bar. Felix didn't drink. Neither did Zed, really. His unique body chemistry processed alcohol too quickly for him to maintain a buzz for longer than a handful of minutes. The bar served simple food, however. Old-fashioned favorites such as hot wings and nachos, and a wide array of snacks designed to keep people nibbling, drinking and socializing. Then there was the view. More polyglass windows, extending the length of the deck. Presently, half of the screens were acting like holo screens. The one closest to them showed a basketball game.

Watching the station teams fight for possession of the ball was about the most relaxing thing Felix had done in the past couple of days, and he could tell Zed enjoyed his pleasure. He kept touching his hand and grinning as if he'd taken a shot of happy juice.

Neither of them needed alcohol.

"Quit it." Felix moved his hand away. "You're being weird." Zed enjoyed his contrariness too.

"Every time Refall Station scores, your heartrate increases."

"Like I said, weird."

The Refall center plucked the ball from the air, stealing it from Xilos. Felix pumped his fist. A mental finger poked his cerebral cortex, sending a mental echo of the cheer down his spine and out along his limbs. Felix gritted his teeth against the almost pain. "Okay, that was worse than weird. Don't do that again."

"Do what?" Zed had both of his hands full of chips and salsa, as though he'd scooped too much on to one and had tried to catch the waterfall of tomato and onion with the other.

"You poked me in the back of the head. I felt it all the way down my spine."

"I didn't—" Zed gagged and dropped his chips to clutch the back of his neck. "What the…ow, fuck."

Felix had his own problems. His crystalline arm had started to hum. He couldn't tell if the sound was audible, or simply a resonance between him and Zed. He grabbed Zed's wrist and their connection slammed into place with a kick. Choking back bile, Felix let go. Beside him, Zed had his hands over his ears and his eyes closed.

They were probably attracting attention. Without bothering to look, Felix tapped at his bracelet, ready to call for medical assistance. Beneath the platinum band, his left wrist ached. His fingers twitched. And he could hear voices.

Hello, hello! HELLO!

Felix met Zed's steel blue gaze. "Can you hear—"

"Yes," Zed ground out. He dropped his hands and patted the air over the table in a gesture no one but Felix understood. Zed had a lot more practice talking to aliens than he did. He had regular conversations with the Guardians, after all. Used to, anyway.

Now, he was trying to tell the resonance to lower their voices.

Closing his eyes, Felix did the same. *Too loud.*

Hello?

Much better. Most resonance had to be reminded about the volume control. They didn't have ears, and they communicated using resonant frequencies that could damage human systems, including biological ones.

Who/where? Felix sent, keeping his mental questions as simple as possible. The resonance didn't have words, either. He'd found communicating with them in terms of spatial relationships worked well. Like swapping engineering plans.

Here!

They didn't actually say that. They sent coordinates. Close coordinates. Felix looked up at Zed. "They're close by."

"Yeah, they're here for the same reason we are." Meaning the *Biswas*, not him and Zed personally, Felix assumed. Zed checked his wallet. "We're about ten hours from show time."

Drift cruisers looped through space in slow arcs. Because they never entered j-space—a folded envelope of reality forming the shortest distance between two points—they tended to confine their routes to a single system or defined region of space, allowing tourists to visit multiple stations, the rare planet marked as viable, and cruise past local phenomena.

The highlight of this cruise would be a close experience with one of the galaxy's most notable nebulae. Spanning twenty light years across, the Eagle Nebula was visible from as far away as Sol, over six thousand light years distant. They weren't much closer. Cruising through a nebula would be about as exciting as pressing your nose to a photograph. The unique clusters of gas and stars were better viewed from afar. They were close enough for the nebula to fill the view screens on one side of the *Biswas*, though, and tonight the polyglass windows would cycle through spectrums of light enhancement, painting the constellations with pretty colors.

The resonance wanted to view the nebula through human technology.

Honor. Zander Emissary. Fluffy Yellow Partner Unit. With. Meet. Resonate.

They wanted to board the *Biswas* and view the show with the two humans their species revered and adored.

Felix hated being revered and adored. He really liked the resonance, though.

It took a bit of maneuvering to arrange an audience with the captain of the *Biswas*, but Zed's name and his former position as the Guardian's emissary smoothed the way. Captain Guan greeted the news of the resonances' request with aplomb, though whether that was a result of inherent captain-ness or the fact that he helmed one of the most exclusive and passenger-centric drifts in human space, Zed didn't know. The rest of the command crew was disciplined enough not to show much emotion, but Zed caught a few nervous glances shared between colleagues. The resonance were still new enough that the galaxy wasn't quite sure of them yet. They certainly seemed threatening, with their massive crystalline forms adorned with all manner of spikes and skewers—unless you could hear their thoughts.

Then it was difficult to think of them as anything but happy puppies.

A few hours later, Zed and Flick awaited the resonance in the docking area. The four hulking figures transitioned through the airlock, happiness and excitement radiating from them. Beside Zed, Captain Guan remained impressively impassive.

"Welcome to the *Biswas*," the captain said.

Smiling, Zed translated.

A low hum emanated from the resonance. *Happy. Joy. Gratitude.*

"They thank you for allowing them to board, Captain. They're pretty excited to be here."

"Of course." A small smile appeared on Guan's lips. "We've cleared a viewing lounge for your use, if you'll follow me?"

Again, Zed passed along the captain's words. Or thoughts that encompassed the words, anyway. It was weird to be communicating in pure concepts again. With Flick, the thoughts they shared were easily interpreted and simplified into words, but without the basis of a shared language with the resonance, it always took a little more effort to get simple ideas across.

They moved into the corridor and Zed was pleased to see that although there were more crewmembers present and crowd-control measures in place, the *Biswas* had not attempted to keep the presence of the resonance a secret. Passengers lined the corridor. A few had their wallets out to take holos while others just stared, eyes wide.

For their part, the resonance seemed unconcerned with the presence of other humans. Zed's connection with them hummed with a constant stream of greeting, which made him smile. He wondered if someday the resonance would come up with a way to communicate without the shards—through sign language, perhaps.

That would be interesting. And freeing.

The lounge was large and completely empty of other passengers, which suited Zed just fine. As much as he appreciated the resonances' desire to make friends, acting as translator was tiring and felt too much like work. But he was looking forward to socializing with them.

Captain Guan saw them seated in front of the polyglass windows, then retreated with a nod. Tension drained out of Flick, and Zed realized his husband had been looking forward to being a translator about as much as he'd been.

The resonance...grew chairs. No matter how many times Zed saw them rearrange their crystalline bodies into another form, he'd never get used to it. They settled onto the floor in front of the windows, and as one, began to resonate. The vibrations sank into Zed's neck, but whereas before, their connection had been overwhelming, this sensation was gentle, welcoming. With a sigh, Zed sank into one of the chairs next to the resonance. Flick took the other one, and threaded the fingers of his crystalline hand through Zed's. Their link thrummed into place, magnifying the hum from the aliens at their side, but it actually felt kind of good.

Fluffy Yellow Partner Unit limb sufficient?

Smiling, Flick extracted his hand from Zed's and held it up, shifting his fingers into another shape, one of the tools he used occasionally. Without touch, Zed couldn't "hear" what Flick said to the resonance, but he felt the aliens' approval and humor.

"Show off," he murmured to Flick.

Flick just smiled and leaned against him. The quiet contentment coming from him was something new, and Zed wondered if his husband was even aware that that now seemed to be his natural state, instead of worry or tension. Zed wasn't sure if their honeymoon was the explanation for the change, or the fact that they'd finally made a decision for themselves, instead of being tossed around by the universe—either way, it didn't matter. It just felt damned good.

The constant hum was almost meditative in nature. Definitely calming. Zed found himself letting go of the nonsense about the stupid porno, letting go of whatever worry he'd had about their ever-increasing damage bills. In the grand scheme, none of that really mattered. He and Flick had fought the universe for their happiness, and they'd won. Happily ever after was bound to come with a few bumps, and a few minor surprises, but that was life.

The lights in the lounge dimmed further, drawing attention to the starscape beyond the window. Slowly, the stars changed from mostly white and yellow to various shades of pink, from magenta all the way to the lightest baby pink. The light and colors seemed to make the nebula dance, teasing out clouds and shapes Zed hadn't seen previously. Over the course of half an hour, the colors transitioned into blue, then green, then purple, orange, yellow, red…it was really quite spectacular. The reverberations from the resonance increased as their pleasure in the show did, and between that and the simple joy of watching pretty lights, Zed hadn't felt so content in ages.

Fluffy Yellow Partner Unit and Zander Emissary resonate strongly. There was a definite sense of approval in the resonances' thoughts.

Thank you, Zed replied. He lifted his arm to wrap it around Flick's shoulders. *He is my reason.* His everything. Zed pressed a kiss to the bouncy blonde curls that had earned Flick his resonance name.

More approval, paired with acceptance, filtered across their link with the aliens. Strange how comforting it felt. For once, Zed decided not to analyze it, and just immerse himself in the moment. He was with new friends, his new husband, enjoying an amazing view.

Life truly didn't get any better.

Chapter Six

So, the nebula show was pretty spectacular. Even pretty. Felix appreciated the fact he lived in a wide and wonderful galaxy, full of mystery and beauty. Sitting with Zed and a unit of resonance throughout the show, though, feeling all of them resonate their feelings about the same thing? Briefly, he wished the rest of the galaxy could get in on this connection thing. It could be weird hearing your lover's thoughts. Being bombarded with impressions of everything from the resonance was wearying. But the thread of belonging woven beneath it all made up for any discomfort. Of being accepted unequivocally as part of the group. Having thoughts thrust into your head because someone was that excited by the process of sharing them with *you*.

If he were the sentimental sort, he'd maybe have to wipe away a tear. Of course, Zed's enigmatic little smile and the gentle brushes of happy, fluffy thought from the resonance meant tears were unnecessary. His thoughts had been received.

On the way back to the docking area, Felix chatted with the smallest of the resonance. The engineer of the unit. Their conversation consisted mostly of an exchange of concepts. Felix knew his arm was limited. He also knew the limit was his imagination, or understanding of the technology. Like when he'd tried to unlock the cargo hatch of the *Chaos* with the touch of a crystalline finger.

According to the engineer—if they understood one another correctly—the idea hadn't been ridiculous. A resonance could have done it. Something about frequency perception and sonic manipulation.

Felix held up a finger and flattened the tip with a thought, making the tool he used most often—a flat head screwdriver. He thinned and lengthened the head, changed the shape, moving through his basic toolbox. He wasn't making an impressive demonstration, though the crew of the *Biswas* seemed interested. Instead, he concentrated on the feeling of the changes. The energy moving through his finger. The source, the purpose. The resonance. Then he paused a transition right in the middle so that his fingertip seemed to shimmer. A bright light sparked upward, then out in a circle of dancing points.

Not what he was trying for.

But beneath, he could feel the change. The vibration.

Resonance, the engineer thought at him. The song of the galaxy.

Nodding, Felix sent back an impression of yellow, which seemed to be the resonances' favorite color, and the way they often expressed happiness.

"Having fun?" Zed was eyeing his bright fingertip with amusement.

Felix touched his fingertip to Zed's cheek and grinned as he felt the resonant feedback as both a mental and physical hum. "Oh yeah. We're going to have fun with this."

He was going to trace every line of musculature on Zed's body with his humming fingertip. Then he'd work on the lock problem. Now, it was time to say goodbye to their guests. The captain of the *Biswas* kept his farewell brief and informal. Felix joined his thoughts to Zed's and sent warmth and contentment and joy. Or, yellow. The resonance ducked back through the airlock.

They'd managed an activity aboard the Biswas without destroying anything.

Then Zed did the diplomatic thing and thanked the captain for his hospitality.

Felix added his bit. "I'm sorry about the room."

"The room?" Captain Guan arched a brow.

"Oh, ah, hmm."

Zed touched his wrist and sent both a *what the fuck are you doing* and laughter.

"Your repair crews are very efficient," Felix said.

The captain's other brow joined the first.

Zed pulled on Felix's wrist. "We've taken enough of your time, captain. Thank you."

"Of course, Mr. Anatolius. If there's anything else I or my crew could do for you, please don't hesitate to let us know. It's an honor to have both of you aboard the *Biswas*."

After a final round of handshakes, they escaped back to their room. The kitchen had been tidied and both 'factors replaced. Felix's experiment had been left behind, however, with all his pieces and parts laid out next to it on a new desk set against the far wall of the living space. Grinning, Felix clapped his hands together.

"Don't even think about it," Zed said.

"What?"

"Those new 'factors are not spare parts. See what's on that new desk? Those are yours. Just those."

"Pffft."

"I'm serious, Flick."

"Okay. I won't take apart the snackfactor. But we don't really need the coffee—"

"Felix."

Felix dredged up a put upon expression, then wrapped his arms around his bulky husband and squeezed. And, because it felt pretty good there all nestled up against Zed's chest, he snuggled in. Just a bit.

Zed wrapped his arms around him. "You being cute is weird and not at all distracting."

"Yeah, but my new magic finger is going to do the trick."

Felix pressed a kiss to Zed's chin, then pulled out of his arms, took his hand and led him to the refurbished bedroom. He'd been half afraid the staff might affix permanent hooks to the headboard, thinking their guests required them. Thankfully, the bedroom looked as bland and somewhat cozy as it had from day one. Someone had folded his clothes and put them away, but otherwise, it still felt like their space.

He pushed Zed toward the bed until he sat, then straddled his lap and kissed him.

Kissing Zed numbered near the top of Felix's list of favorite things to do. Sex was awesome. So was sleep. He could lose himself in a good project for hours. Nothing quite compared to the feeling of coming home that swept through him every time he touched his lips to Zed's, though. Kisses were so intimate. An invitation to taste and share. A confirmation. Connection.

As always, their mental link snapped into being. Felix sent no thoughts, he merely reveled in the feeling of being surrounded by his lover. Then, pulling back, he kissed Zed's chin and jawline. Moved along to nibble at an earlobe. Nipped and licked at his neck. Beneath him, Zed sighed and moaned. He had his hands wrapped around Felix's back, his lips fastened to Felix's neck. The moment was perfect.

And perfect only needed a moment. They were here to play.

"Shirt off," Felix instructed.

Zed unwrapped his arms and tugged his shirt over his head. Felix ignited the tip of a crystalline finger so it hummed with light and touched it to one of Zed's nipples, right below the piercing. Zed...keened.

"Is that a good sound or a bad sound?"

"It's a..." Zed licked his lips and took a breath. "Fuck, I could feel that in my balls. It was good and weird and so fucking good. Do it again."

Felix shuffled back off Zed's lap. "Lie back."

Zed kicked off his shoes and scooted back along the bed. Felix gestured toward his pants. "Might as well get rid of those too."

"Is this your fantasy? Ordering me about?"

"No. Maybe? You seem to like it." Zed often gave him a look that begged for instruction. Felix treated it like a game, not as a fantasy to indulge. He liked that Zed let him take charge in bed. He liked that Zed trusted him. Touching Zed's knee, he sent a tendril of thought to explain his feeling on the subject.

Zed returned a vague nod. "You don't want to go back to the fantasy suites."

"No."

"Are you sure?"

"Do you?" Felix asked.

"I thought I did, but—"

"I could see us maybe having fun in a pirate ship holo or something. But, honestly, Zed? I don't want to have sex with you in a holo suite. I don't need to. You're..." Oh, wow, he hadn't been about to just say that, had he?

"I'm what? Are you blushing?"

"No."

"You are so blushing. Oh my God. Your ears are bright red!"

Growling, Felix bent to pick up the discarded shirt. Zed scooted forward so he sat on the edge of the bed again and grabbed at Felix's hand. "It's cute."

"What is this thing you have with cute today? I'm in no way, shape or form, cute."

Zed's smile broadened to a grin.

"Fine. You're my fantasy, okay? Just you. As you are. All big and muscly and a hero and letting me have my way with you, make love to you..." Could you do yourself an injury blushing?

"C'mere." Zed pulled him in close. "Love you."

Felix did his best impression of a Betan yarl for a second or two, thinking prickly and thorny thoughts. Then he softened and dropped a kiss to Zed's cheek. "Love you too. Now, do you want me to tease you with my magic finger or not?"

"Want." Zed sent a spike of need through the connection.

"Then we better finish getting undressed."

Shoes thumped to the floor and clothing fluttered down on top of them. Then Felix knelt on the bed next to Zed and leaned in for a kiss. Zed tasted of lust and love. Felix added his desire to the mix, and his love. The endless, boundless well of it. His certainty that what they had was everything.

Always and forever.

Sometimes, Flick had the best ideas. And he was absolutely right. They didn't need a fancy room or fantasies. They didn't need to tie each other up or banter dirty talk back and forth—though Zed would be the first to admit it had been hot as fuck. All they needed was each other. Their lips, their hands, their bodies.

He arched into the kiss, looking for some more friction anywhere. Anywhere at all. Flick chuckled against his lips and drew back, smiling. "Impatient."

"Horny," Zed countered.

Still grinning, Flick bent forward to nibble at Zed's neck, trailing toward his chest. The little nips drove Zed mad—they were so good, but not nearly enough. A zing against his nipple ring reminded him of Flick's new trick and he groaned, pressing his head back into the pillow. Flick knew all the buttons to push, all the notes to hit.

Flick's human thumb rubbed the tip of Zed's cock, smearing the drop of liquid there. He looked...kind of like a conquering king, kneeling on the bed beside Zed, intent, focused, and grinning evilly. "You really like that, huh?"

"Really do."

"Awesome." Before Zed knew what he was doing, Flick dragged his magic finger along his cock.

"Shit!" Zed whimpered—he couldn't help it. The touch didn't hurt, far from it. It was just intense. As Flick swept his finger up and down the sensitive skin, Zed swore he got harder. He squirmed and shifted, not really trying to get away, but unable to stay still. It was as though Flick's finger was a vibrator, buzzing along his skin—but reaching inside, too. Resonating with his cock.

It was fucking incredible.

"Are you gonna come?" Flick asked breathlessly.

"Don't—" Zed broke off with a groan. "Don't think so. Not like this." A couple of good strokes, though...

"But it's good?"

"*Fuck*, yes."

"What if I do this?" Flick's finger abandoned Zed's erection to travel further south, and Zed opened his legs further in anticipation and invitation.

His balls were almost too sensitive for the treatment, something Flick must have picked up on because he didn't linger there. Instead, his finger dipped behind Zed's balls and softly stroked, the resonance making Zed bite his lip and moan. He was hardly thinking when he drew his legs up and held them behind his knees, giving Flick all the room he could possibly want.

"Oh yeah." Flick pushed up Zed's knee a little more so he could maneuver in between his legs. "There we go. You need any prep?"

With how often they'd been having sex over the past few days? "Nope, I'm good."

Flick grabbed the lube and slicked himself up, then brushed more against Zed's hole. It was so tempting to let go of one of his legs and have a stroke—he wasn't quite on the cusp of orgasm yet, but it wouldn't take much to get there. Need and want and horniness thrummed through him, though he wasn't sure where his thoughts ended and Flick's began.

The head of Flick's cock pressed against Zed's ass, then slowly, slowly edged inside. God, yes. Zed let his head fall back, reveling in the sensation of being stretched and filled. Their connection snapped into place, even stronger than a moment ago, and Zed let the thoughts and emotions wash over him, taking away the last of his coherent thought.

Too soon, not soon enough, Flick was fully inside of him. He met Flick's gaze for a moment, noting that Flick seemed just as breathless as Zed was.

"Yeah?" Flick asked.

"Yeah."

Flick didn't need any further invitation. He leaned over Zed, his crystalline hand gripping Zed's hip and his human hand braced on the bed, and thrust.

They knew every one of each other's tells now. The signs to speed up, the signs to slow down. When they should slam their bodies together as hard and fast as possible, and when they should make love slowly, easily. Tonight wasn't a slow and easy night— Flick had gotten Zed too worked up for that. He hooked a hand behind Flick's neck and tugged him down for a sloppy, urgent kiss.

"Harder," he whispered.

"Demanding." Flick pulled out, leaving Zed gasping, and tapped Zed's hip. "Over."

Grinning, Zed got to his hands and knees. Flick slid back home without hesitation, and proceeded to give Zed exactly what he'd asked for. Hard, harder—and with every stroke, Flick hit his prostate, making his whole body light up. Zed's head drooped as he pushed back into each of Flick's thrusts, taking him as deep as he could.

"So good," he slurred.

Flick's only answer was a grunt—but then a hand surrounded Zed's dick, and he couldn't help his shout of surprise. Flick stroked in time with his thrusts, and Zed was almost...almost...

"Fuck!" Colors exploded across his vision as he came, hard, his whole body tensing up. Caught up in his own shudders and waves of climax, he was barely aware of Flick finding his own release.

His arms and legs suddenly gave out, sending them both sprawling to the bed. Flick nuzzled the nape of his neck and chuckled. "Wimp."

"I am officially fucked out," Zed said into the pillow.

After a second, Flick shifted to lie beside him and poked and prodded until Zed rolled onto his back, making room for cuddling. Zed didn't bother to hide his smile, and Flick huffed at him even as he tucked himself against Zed's broader form.

There really wasn't anything better than lying in bed, totally sated—even if there was a bit of a wet spot—with his husband's mop of curls tickling his chest, Zed decided. Not a damned thing. He pressed a kiss to Flick's hair, then let himself drift, enjoying the post-orgasm light show put on by his wacky brain chemistry.

Fifteen minutes or an hour could have passed when Flick suddenly stiffened beside him. Zed jerked fully awake. "What?"

"I figured it out. If I switch out the capacitor, and do a different connection...then reflect that change in the code..."

Zed angled himself up to look at Flick. "What are you talking about?"

"The 'factor. Oh my God, why didn't I see it before? It makes perfect sense. And it would increase the output by…" Flick let his words trail off. "Sorry. I shouldn't—you're right, no more tinkering." Flick rolled on his side, closer to Zed, and closed his eyes.

Zed didn't need their connection to tell him that Flick's mind hadn't stopped spinning, though. He sighed. "Go."

Flick popped up. "Really?"

"I have two stipulations. One—don't blow anything up. Two—use the desk, okay? Save your back."

"Done and done. Okay. I've totally got this." Without a look back, Flick scrambled out of bed and into the living area, still naked. He probably wouldn't notice he was naked, either, until a spark landed somewhere unpleasant.

Sighing happily, Zed tucked his hands under his head and watched colors play across the ceiling. He drifted off to sleep to the sound of Flick's tinkering and low curses—maybe not the most romantic thing to an outsider looking in, but to Zed, it was perfect. It was the essence of the man he'd married, and he wouldn't change it for anything in the galaxy.

EXTRAS

There is so much more we'd like to share with you all. To round out this volume, we've included two cut scenes and a couple of our favourite posts—Chaos Station trivia and an interview with the guys.

Snakes on a Ship

To celebrate the launch of Phase Shift, *the last book in the Chaos Station series, we dug out at a scene from* Lonely Shore *that didn't make the final cut. Elias, Zed and Felix were trying to off-load some ill-gotten wine to a questionable buyer on an even more questionable station.*

They paused outside a shaded window and, as one, lifted their chins so they could read the holo floating just over the door.

"Renenutet's Emporium," Zed said.

"Sounds Ashushk," Felix said.

"More Egyptian," Elias countered.

"Yeah?" Felix scratched his head, his finger still encountering little more than soft stubble. How long did hair take to grow anyway? "Well, so long as it's got nothing to do with moths and cartels, it's all good."

"Snakes," Elias said.

"Huh?"

"Renenutet was an Egyptian goddess who appeared as a hooded cobra." Elias nodded toward the flattened snake head symbol pressed into the molding over the columns flanking the door.

"That has got to be the most obscure fact in your head," Felix said.

Zed looked at Elias as if he waited for the captain to either refute the statement, or produce another obscure fact. Instead, Elias just grinned. "Yeah, it's pretty out there." He looked back at the door. "If a woman with a snake head greets us inside, though, I'm gone."

Right. Elias didn't like snakes, which was probably why he had a head stuffed with oddball facts about them.

The interior of the emporium was almost disappointing. No snake-headed goddesses floated out from dark corners and no tattooed gangsters leapt up from behind the counter. Instead, an old man stood, patting a frail hand across the dusty countertop in front of him. He located an old-fashioned looking pair of spectacles, slipped them over his beak of a nose and looked up. His eyes, magnified by the convex glass, blinked owlishly at each of them in turn. A pink tongue dragged across curiously fleshy lips as he returned his attention to Zed.

"Captain Idowu?" The old man's gaze roamed across Zed's broad shoulders, down his flanks, centered and rose again.

Cheeks dusky with a faint blush, Zed pointed toward Elias.

The captain took a step forward. "Mr. Renen?"

"Indeed." Renen's magnified gaze hadn't left Zed. "You're a big fellow, aren't you?"

Elias's shoulders twitched, as if he resisted the urge to lean into the path of the old man's gaze. Instead, he introduced the big fellow. "My security officer, Mr. Loop." By agreement, they didn't use Zed's real name in places where it might stir up more than dust. Elias waved in Felix's direction. "And my engineer, Mr. Ingesson."

Renen continued to study Zed. "Nice to make your acquaintance, Mr. Loop."

Zed offered a brusque nod in return. The color on his cheeks had narrowed from a blush to annoyed spots. Renen spared a quick glance for Elias and an even shorter pass of Felix before returning his attention to Zed, apparently oblivious to, or excited by, the veiled threat of the larger man's expression. "You have some wine for me?"

Elias made a small noise in the back of his throat, which was unnoticed by Renen. Felix swallowed the beginnings of a chuckle as Zed reached up to tug at the collar of his grey shirt. Imagine if he'd worn black. Renen's large eyes followed the movement and his myopic gazed fixed on Zed's chest. Felix nudged Zed's ribs and jerked his head toward the hovering sleds of wine. Apparently negotiation was the sexy security officer's job today.

Zed cleared his throat and said, "Twelve dozen bottles of Risus varietals. They tend toward the more full-bodied grape. Shiraz, claret, Bordeaux-style. A dozen Malbec in there too."

Renen spared a glance for the crates, then quickly looked back at Zed, lifting his white whiskered chin so he could meet the soldier's eyes. "You seem to know your wine, sir."

Feeling evil, Felix grinned. "Mr. Loop has a keen appreciation for the finer things, Mr. Renen." Which was nothing but the truth.

"Indeed." Renen pushed his spectacles up his nose and rounded the counter so he could sidle up to Zed. "And your asking price?"

"Was in the sales form we forwarded," Elias put in.

Renen flicked an annoyed glance in Elias direction. "But not a final figure."

"No," Elias confirmed.

Between them, the *Chaos* crew had settled on a lowest sum they'd take for the wine. Felix could sense Elias subtracting zeroes from that figure now, anything to shorten the deal and pull Zed out from under. Zed, who'd made a heroic effort to stand still beneath the scrutiny of the ancient lecher, probably wouldn't fight it. Felix, who cared little for credits, would happily abandon the crates…after he'd watched his lover squirm just a little more.

"We'll take three hundred per crate," Zed said.

"Oh, I've something else in mind."

Felix swallowed a chuckle and it hurt, damn it. He reached up to massage his neck and Elias looked over, his eyes shining with mirth. Felix shook his head and Elias put a hand to his mouth, ostensibly to rub at his chin. Zed's shoulders stiffened.

Zed could flirt. A crook of his lips and Felix was his…utterly. No surprise there. But one look from his steel-blue eyes could melt the resistance of even the iciest bitch. He used his power with discretion, however, as if he figured he might actually have to follow up at some point, and while his taste was wide and varied, it did not include wizened old gentlemen. Ever.

"What would that be?" Zed asked, his tone carefully neutral.

"An even trade. I have a shipment of Vernese Pythons that will fetch three hundred credits each, maybe more."

Elias' shoulders lined up with Zed's. "A shipment of what?" he asked.

Renen produced a wallet, folded it open and tapped. A blank wall, one that had previously garnered no more attention than it warranted, began to slide into the floor. Behind, stacked in four rows of three were a dozen Perspex cubes holding twelve snakes. Big snakes. Fucking huge snakes, massive coils pressed up against the thick plastic. Through the series of pinprick ventilation holes that marked the upper edge of each cube, a chorus of hisses slithered through the air, a soft susurrus that caressed the ear and the fine hairs along the back of the neck.

Felix's stomach cramped as he shivered. He didn't have a particular phobia of snakes, but reckoned twelve—whose bodies ranged from the thickness of his thigh to Zed's—were eleven too many. Twelve too many. Shit, Elias was going to—

"Nope." The captain backed into Felix and edged around him toward the door. "No deal, no sale. No way, no how. No snakes on the *Chaos*, not now, not ever."

Zed turned to his captain, a glint of evil lighting his cool blue eyes. "They're in cubes, Eli. Perfectly safe."

Elias glared at his security officer. "Ever seen that old vid? *Snakes on a Plane*? It's a fucking disaster waiting to happen, man, and it ain't happening on my boat."

Zed cocked his head to one side. "We could sell these for twice what he's giving them to us for."

Wrapping a hand around Zed's meaty forearm, Renen inserted himself into the conversation. "Oh, indeed. It's a fair trade for me. The wine is much easier to sell on station than the snakes. A deal we can both profit from." He rubbed Zed's arm.

Zed smacked his hand away. "You might have mentioned the snakes in your initial communication."

The snakes hissed.

"But I prefer to deal in person. It's so much more pleasant, don't you think?" He gazed up at Zed. "We might never have had the chance to meet otherwise."

Oh, God.

"Never going to happen, Renen," Zed said through gritted teeth. Then a large hand hooked Felix around the neck and pulled him in close. "See this man?" Zed paused, then looked at Felix and smiled, his cheeks lifting and his eyes warming. "He is all I need." He leaned in and pressed a kissed to Felix's lips.

While flattered to be possessed so thoroughly in the company of a stranger, Felix couldn't relax into the kiss. Not because he felt Zed had used him as an excuse. Nope, he'd take any opportunity to be Zed's. Made him feel better than good, a glow that started somewhere around his toes and worked its way slowly upward. More, the hissing of the damned snakes cut into the moment. Leeched the joy out of his fucking joy. Elias panicking behind him sorta ruined it, too, and the way Renen kept licking his lips.

And the fact they were obviously going to be trailed back to the *Chaos* by two sleds of wine.

Still, it was moment and Felix tucked it away into the core of his being. He'd take it out and hug it later. Stretch it, play with it, love it quietly.

Therapy

While this scene was cut from Skip Trace *during the developmental edit phase, it wasn't cut from Felix and Zander's story. In between* Skip Trace *and* Inversion Point *Zander and Felix kept regular appointments with Dr. McMann. This scene is the first such appointment and probably occurs very shortly after the events of* Skip Trace.

"Good morning, Zander."

Dr. McMann's pleasant, melodic voice cut through the tension that permeated her office. Zed tried to let it wash away the weight that had his shoulders bunched and curved, but Flick fidgeted beside him, and his muscles knotted again.

"Good morning, Doctor." He smiled, but it didn't feel very steady on his lips. "This is Felix Ingesson, my, uh…"

"His," Flick said.

Amusement flashed over the doctor's features. "Lovely to meet you, Felix." She waved to the couch. "Please, have a seat."

Zed sat, pressing his thigh against Flick's. The engineer vibrated, his leg bouncing. His hands alternately clenched into fists, then gripped together. He might as well have been yelling *fuck no* at the top of his lungs…yet he hadn't tried to get out of this appointment and he wasn't making any real attempts to leave now. Zed dropped his hand to Flick's leg to get it to stop bouncing and the engineer's mangled palm slapped down over top of it.

Dr. McMann settled into one of the chairs across from the couch. "And how are you two doing?"

"Good," Zed said quickly. "I mean, not perfect, but…good."

"I'm glad to hear it. And I'm glad Felix decided to accompany you today."

Flick snorted and a corner of his lips curved upward for a breath.

"Even if he isn't," the doctor said with a chuckle. "At the end of our last session, Zander, I asked you to think about what you want and work on giving yourself permission to want it and have it. Did you manage that?"

Zed huffed out a breath. On the one hand, he was thankful that the doctor seemed to grasp that Flick didn't want to be the focus of this session—that wasn't Zed's intention in bringing him here. On the other, he'd kind of hoped she'd forgotten about his homework. "Yes and no," he hedged. "You heard the news, right?"

"That you were arrested? Yes," she said quietly. She watched him for a moment. "As cliché as the question is, how did that make you feel?"

Betrayed, disillusioned, hurt, depressed...he could put so many words to it, and yet none of them quite covered the gamut of emotions. "My entire life, I had one goal," he said, looking at his lap instead of meeting the doctor's eyes or being tempted to glance at Flick. "I wanted to serve. I wanted to be in the AEF. I wanted to explore, I wanted to protect people, I just...I..."

"You wanted to be a hero," Flick offered, his voice barely audible.

Soft laughter escaped Zed's lips on a breath. "Yeah."

"It's a noble goal," Dr. McMann said.

"It was a stupid goal. I mean, how fucking naïve could I be? How didn't I see that the AEF didn't give a fuck? I was blind, so damned blind, and...God, I'm not a hero. I was never a hero."

"The civilians you rescued would argue that," Dr. McMann said.

"That was one action. One. Out of thousands."

"And some of those weren't as heroic?"

Zed gritted his teeth. "No. There was one..." He glanced at Flick, knowing why his mind ventured to this particular dark spot on a regular basis. "My team's assignment was to infiltrate a colony the stin had overrun. Dark drop, a thousand klicks out, and we had to make our way to the settlement. Ever see pics or vids of the colonies the stin attacked, Doc? They don't destroy buildings, if they can help it. See, people might get trapped inside, and that means the stin can't fight them one on one."

"I know," Dr. McMann said, her voice steady. Of course she'd know—he wasn't the first soldier to seek her out for post-war treatment. "Go on."

"We walked into the town, and there were bodies everywhere. Men, women, children, fucking animals. The stin don't care who they sink their claws into, as long as they get to do it." Zed was aware that the doctor's office had faded, that he was falling into memories, but he couldn't stop it. "We were waiting in an alley, me and my partner for the mission, when we saw a stin walk by. Once it was past, I almost stepped out into the road, but then I saw movement.

"It was a slave, a human slave. I'd heard the rumors that the stin sometimes kept pets. Trophies. We knew there were work camps, too. He was shuffling along behind the stin, like he was on a leash."

He could still remember the flash of hope he'd felt, even if at the time he'd refused to acknowledge it—and then the crash of emotion as he remembered that Flick was dead, that he wouldn't be walking along a street on a colony on the ass-end of nowhere. He rubbed his chest at the memory of the ache in his heart.

"The slave saw me. He opened his mouth to alert the stin. So I drew my knife and sank it into his throat." Zed's jaw flexed and he closed his eyes, keeping his head down. "I killed him."

"Your mission had to take priority."

"Fuck the mission," Zed spat. "There was no one left on the colony to save except him, that one guy. I killed him in favor of laying bombs to make a stupid and totally ineffectual point. And..." He closed his eyes tighter.

"And what, Zander?"

Zed stayed silent for a long minute, the doctor's question echoing, as he gathered the courage to answer it. "And what if it had been Flick?" he breathed.

"Would you have done the same thing?"

"I don't know." God, he wanted to grab for Flick's hand and squeeze it, but he doubted Flick wanted to touch him just then. "I want to say no."

"But you can't."

"No, I can't." He forced his eyes open and looked at Flick. "I'm sorry. I'm so sorry."

Not what he expected.

If he sweated anymore, his body would collapse, all husk-like. And dead. If he continued to fidget, he'd wear through the reinforced seams of his pants—a challenge he might just have set for himself. Felix had expected the stomach cramps and the whole feeling like a stranger in his skin thing. He remembered that from his last visit with a shrink, four years or so ago. Back then. Back when he'd been pulled lovingly back into the embrace of the AEF and charged with desertion, piracy and treason.

Fuckers.

Felix closed his eyes, blocking out Zed's face. The pain, the guilt, the horror, the need in that gray-blue gaze. Not what he had expected.

The one rational brain cell in his head piped up with a simple song: *Forgive him.* It wasn't Zed's fault. None of it had been Zed's fault. Even if Zed hadn't walked away from him after graduation, they'd probably still be here, sitting on this not-so-comfortable couch, basking in the not-so-soothing attention of Dr. What's-her-face.

Opening his eyes, Felix caught her gaze, searched it and quickly found what he looked for: excitement.

What sort of person thrived on the pain of others?

Fucking parasite.

This had been a bad idea.

Before his thighs could break contact with the couch, that one brain cell rallied a few others and declared martial law. Zed needed this, maybe more than he did. Anger, raw and brutal, swept through Felix. His limbs trembled with it, his psyche vibrated. He knew Zed and the doctor could see him shake. He knew they figured Zed's cold and calculated kill was the cause. It was, but not for the reason they thought. Oh, no. It was much more complicated than that. And it was damned hard to think with rage trickling into his brain, shaking everything up.

The doctor opened her mouth. Before she could ask anyone how shit made them feel, Felix pointed a crooked finger at her. "Don't."

To her credit, she didn't blanch.

He turned to Zed. "They don't want heroes. They want tools. And when they break them, they toss them…us aside." He couldn't be telling Zed anything he didn't know, right? Felix gestured toward the doctor. "Tell her what you want. What you think you can't have."

Zed's throat moved as he swallowed, the sound tight, the movement probably painful. Felix remembered that, too, from his last visit with a professional. Hell, his throat dried up every time he had to admit he'd made a mistake, or that he'd had an emotion other than self-pity. Hadn't always been that way. For three and a half years… Okay, for maybe three years, he'd been all right. Not solid, but good enough. Then Zed had walked back into his life. Felix didn't understand why the one thing he wanted more than any other had to cost so much, but looking into Zed's gray eyes, he figured he wasn't the only one struggling to pay the debt.

How had they ever imagined they could just pick up where they left off?

Zed spoke, and the single word, the choked-up little cough, sounded like "you."

Felix sucked in a breath and held it.

"It's you, Flick. I want a life with you."

Felix breathed out. The back of his eyes burned, but he didn't blink. Lord knows, that would only encourage the tears nestling in his ducts. "Good," he said, his single-word answer equally choked.

"I can't save you," Zed said.

"I know." Felix blinked and his vision blurred a little. God, he wanted Zed to save him. He'd wanted it…forever. Since he was eight years old and had his skinny fingers wrapped around the fat wallet of the glossy-haired and rosy-cheeked swank. He'd wanted someone to make his mother well, to restore his father's arm and pride, to keep his sister out of the back alleyways. And, he supposed he'd wanted that someone to be him. Every little boy wanted to be a hero, didn't he? But then Zed had just…happened. The credits in that wallet had kept his mother in meds for six months, giving her time to build strength. The scholarship that gave Felix his education had allowed him to move his family out of the bowels of the station, up one level to where the apartments had two rooms…and walls. His career had given him the resources to replace his father's arm.

Felix looked down at his mangled left hand. The irony failed to amuse him. "We all wanted to die. At some point, we all wanted to die. That slave…" He looked up again, which required effort as his head felt heavy. "You did him a favor. A quick, clean death." He couldn't touch Zed's question, the one that obviously plagued the former soldier, so he told his own story instead. "I had a friend in the colony, a woman I looked after. She was small and sick. Always sick." She'd reminded him of his mother. "We had a quota every shift and I helped fill hers. I gave her my food, too." He scoffed. "Not that that was a favor. They fed us this paste—this crunchy, bitter shit. I think it was squashed up roaches or something."

Felix paused to fill his lungs. His head spun lightly and that one rational brain cell swelled up and throbbed. Or maybe he just had a headache. He worked his jaw, seeking to ease the tension in his neck, and winced at the series of clicks and grates. Zed stroked his knuckles again and the doctor remained blessedly silent.

"I always filled her truck before mine and one day I didn't get mine finished." He pushed his hand further into Zed's lap. "So they crushed my hand." A hissing gasp wafted over from the direction of the doctor. "Makes no sense, right? To break me so that I couldn't work as efficiently. Unless they wanted to make it so I could only fill one truck a day, so I couldn't cooperate with my fellow slaves. Keep a friend."

Tears ran freely down Zed's cheeks. His expression remained stoic, however, as if he knew if he crumbled, Felix would fall apart.

"They killed her, too." And left her body to rot in the mines, just as they did the bodies of all who fell. Felix didn't pass that putrid little morsel along, though. The doc looked ready to pass out and Zed didn't need another cross to bear. "I don't know what the point of my story is, I just..." He breathed out, shoulders shifting down.

"We can't always save those who need saving. Who we think need saving," the doctor said.

Felix glanced over at her. "If you ask me how that makes me feel, I'm going to tear this office apart. And then you might have an idea."

She nodded.

Zed squeezed his hand gently. "I'm sorry."

Shaking his head, Felix turned their hands over so their palms could meet. The tattoo on the inside of Zed's wrist caught his eye and Felix extended his fingers toward it. "It's okay." Didn't feel okay, not really. But that impending sense of doom had eased back a little. He could breathe. His skin didn't itch and his heart didn't ache. "I'll be okay." Zed's hand wrapped around his and held tight. Felix breathed into the warm and quiet moment and then looked up at the doctor again. "We 'bout done here?"

"I think that's enough for today, yes."

"I don't do homework. Give that to Zander. He was always a good student."

Zed's mouth twitched. "So were you. In fact, I seem to remember—"

Felix waved his good hand through the air. "Don't ruin my image, man, or she'll expect me to come here and actually talk. I planned to do the broody silence thing until she got bored."

"She has a name, Flick."

Dr. McMann. And he was being rude. Felix glanced over again and saw about what he expected. Not amusement, but a tolerant humor. She'd met his type before and she'd probably bested them. Trust Zed to pick the best fucking shrink. She wasn't unpleasant to look at, either.

"Felix."

He lifted his gaze from her boobs—they didn't do much for him, but they were all nicely rounded and shit.

"There is no blueprint for this."

Yep, she had him pegged.

"And I don't bore easily."

He flicked his gaze away and tried not to smile. Standing up, he smoothed the loosened threads on his pants so that they appeared less ragged. "I'm gonna wait out in the…" He waved at the door. "Whatever so y'all can talk about something other than me." He'd co-opted enough of Zed's session. Glancing at Dr. McMann, he dipped his chin, giving her a quick nod. It wasn't the most polite gesture, but she seemed to take it for what it was—all he could offer right now.

Outside, he prowled the waiting area, ignoring couches that weren't quite plush and not quite sensible. He didn't *get* the feel of the office, what the décor meant, what vibe it was supposed to give off, but he did appreciate that it didn't interfere with his stride, or his thoughts. Nothing poked at him. Zed stepped out of the inner sanctum a short while later and stood close by, but not too close, as if he suspected Felix might explode.

Felix stopped his pacing. "I know your dad paid for the Academy." Zed opened his mouth and Felix employed a bent finger, pointing him into silence. "I also know he considered it an investment rather than a gift." He lifted his shoulders. "Who knows what he thinks of the return. But that's not why I'm here, why I've always been…" Would it be corny to put his hand over his heart? Felix did it anyway, pressing his palm flat to the front of his shirt. "Here. For you. You make me want to be a better man, Zander. You always have. I've always wanted to measure up, be your equal. I know I don't need a shitload of credits to qualify, or a face that makes your heart skip or whatever. I just want to be with you because..." Fuck. "This is going to sound stupid."

"Nothing you say is stupid."

He'd counter that later, when his snark returned.

Felix moved his hand to Zed's shirt, let his fingers curl into the soft silk. "You're my hero, Zed. Always have been, always will be."

Zed pulled him into a fast, hard hug, crushing him against his massive chest. Air puffed out of Felix's lungs, but that was okay. He didn't need it, not right then, not when it might have otherwise emerged on a sob. Tucking his head into Zed's shoulder, he leaned in and hugged back. Hard.

"Love you." Zed's whisper ruffled his hair.

Felix squeezed him just a bit tighter. "Love you too."

Zed's hold loosened and both their chests heaved with the effort of drawing in a full breath. Felix stepped back a little and rolled his shoulders.

"Let's go break stuff," he said.

"Want to hit the gym at the Damianos Building?"

"Yes."

Once the clamor of the concourse outside the suite wrapped around them, Felix said, "We can talk about the rest of it later, 'kay?"

Zed offered a short, sharp nod. Then, a smile. A feral and sorta sexy smile. "We'll beat the shit out of some of Bren's recruits. Or a kick bag. Or each other."

"Or all three."

"Then we'll fuck."

Felix grinned.

"And then we'll talk."

"It's a deal."

Interview with AllSpace Alliance News

I'm Tanis Nejem for AllSpace Alliance News. With me today are Zander Anatolius and Felix Ingesson. Welcome, both of you.

Zed: Nice to see you again, Tanis.

Felix: *mumble*

Zander is perhaps best known as Emissary to the Guardians. Before retiring from the Allied Earth Forces, Mr. Anatolius held the rank of major and commanded a team of dedicated individuals who unquestionably turned the tide of the Human-Stin War. Since, he's been branded both a hero and a traitor. With the details of Project Dreamweaver come to light, it seems clear the men and woman recruited to the project were betrayed by the very organization they held dear, the AEF.

Felix also served with the AEF until he was captured by the stin in 2261 and declared KIA shortly thereafter. Obviously very much alive, Mr. Ingesson's status was reversed after he escaped from stin custody and made his way back to human space. The information he shared with the AEF regarding his capture and imprisonment undoubtedly resulted in the repatriation of thousands of AEF personnel.

Zander...may I call you Zander? It's been two months since you were released from AEF custody and cleared of all charges. How are you?

Zed: I'm doing well, Tanis. Thank you for asking.

And you, Felix?

Felix: *fidgets* I'm good.

How is your relationship with the AEF these days?

Felix: Unhealthy.

Zed: I think what Felix means is that our latest…um, encounters with the AEF have not cast them in the most favorable light.

Well, we can tell who's done interviews before. That's a very diplomatic answer.

Zed: I realize that, but what good will it do for me to rage about past events. None. The AEF doesn't particularly like me anymore, and I'm not its biggest fan either. Let's move on.

I'm sure I'm not the only one who'd love to know how you two met. Was it aboard the *Chaos*?

Felix: We met surfing the rings of Saturn.

Zed: *glares at Felix* We met when we were kids, actually. I befriended Felix on a visit to his home station of Pontus and later on, he won a scholarship to Shepard Academy, where we roomed together.

So you were friends first?

Zed: Best friends. No one knew me better than Felix—and that's still the truth.

Felix: *fights a smile*

As a result of the war, you didn't see one another for eight
years.

Felix: Nearly nine.

Zed: We entered different branches of the military. Then—

Felix: I got killed.

Ah—

Zed: Reported as MIA, then KIA when the wreckage of the
McCandless was recovered. *clasps Felix's knee* But it's hard to
kill Felix.

Felix: Hard to kill you too.

Right, the Guardians intervened when you were taken to
Ashushk Prime.

Zed: *tight smile*

Felix: *tight smile*

Zander, you've communicated more and spent more time
with the Guardians than anyone else in the galaxy. What can
you share about them?

Zed: Honestly, not much. I've never seen a Guardian. I think I
was aboard one of their ships, but I couldn't tell you for certain.
They are just as mysterious to me as they are to everyone else.

What does your role as Emissary entail?

Zed: I'm their voice. The Guardians believe in free will, but they also want the species of the galaxy to know that they're here. At the same time, they realize that their presence is not always the right solution. So I'm to act as their representative when their presence would overshadow the matter at hand.

Are you in regular contact with the Guardians?

Zed: I wouldn't say regular, no. They contact me as they see fit.

Have you ever had contact with the Guardians, Felix?

Felix: We've had words.

Any you can share?

Felix: *turns to Zed* No comment.

Zed: This isn't a press conference, Flick.

Felix: I know that. But I'm still not going to share. Talking to the Guardians isn't something anyone should take lightly.

What's this I hear about the Church of Omega? Do you have an official stance on them?

Felix: *murmurs* Kill 'em all and let their collection of useless gods sort them out.

Zed: *clears his throat* They're...enthusiastic. But misguided. My official stance is that neither I nor the crew of the *Chaos* is affiliated with the Church in any way and I have no interest in them.

You two met up again when Zander hired the *Chaos* to help track a bounty. How was it seeing one another after so long, after all that had happened?

Felix: No comment.

Zed: Flick—

Felix: I think anyone with a single iota of imagination can fill in the blanks on that one.

Zed: It was a bit of a surprise.

Felix: Yeah, like the Human-Stin War was a bit of a problem.

Are you a permanent member of the crew now, Zander?

Zed: Yes. I have no plans to be anywhere else than with the *Chaos*.

How did you acquire the other members of your crew?

Felix: We don't. We're full. We don't want any more crew.

Zed: You mean Elias, Nessa and Qek?

Felix: Oh. No comment.

Zed: *sigh, nudges Felix*

Felix: Fine, whatever. I originally worked with Elias on his father's ship. Then we decided to buy our own and go into business together. Qek and Nessa were a matched set. That's it, nothing really complicated about it.

What sort of goods do you carry?

Felix: Shit, mostly. Want some?

Zed: Whatever the contract calls for. Within reason, I mean. The *Chaos* can't take really large loads.

Felix: Or livestock. Elias draws the line at livestock.

Zed: Especially snakes.

Felix: *snickers*

What does your family think of your involvement with the Guardians, Zander?

Zed: What would anyone's family think? They're concerned. Puzzled. Not entirely sure what to make of it.

Felix: Well, we've got that in common.

What about your family, Felix? I understand you're from Pontus Station.

Felix: Pontus Station was pretty much destroyed by the stin. Next question.

There were many surv—

Felix: Next question.

Zed: *nudges Felix's shoulder* Felix's family is the Anatolius clan. And the crew of the *Chaos*. Let's move on.

Your family has always been in the limelight, Zander, but you managed to mostly avoid it until the incident on Engandini where you and your team were filmed rescuing a civilian transport. And now with this newest development, you're back in the spotlight. How does it feel?

Zed: I'm not a fan.

I would have thought it would be a return to normal for you.

Zed: Not really. I was never as in the spotlight as the rest of my family, and during the war, I was in covert ops. Meaning I was not supposed to be in the media in any way. So this scrutiny...

Felix: He doesn't like it.

Felix, you've been pretty free with your fists and the media. Have there been any repercussions?

Felix: *balls fists before making a visible effort to relax them* Yes.

Would you elaborate for us?

Felix: Broken noses, bloody mouths. At least one concussion.

Zed: *makes a noise in his throat*

Felix: Fine. The repercussions are questions like this. The media doesn't like me and the feeling is mutual.

I think you'd be surprised.

Felix: Y'all should just concentrate on Zed. He's the pretty one.

Zed: Nah, Flick, it's your blond curls. No one can resist them.

What's next for you two? Any wedding bells in the future?

Felix: No comment.

Zed: *grasps Felix's hand* We're taking things day by day, finding a new normal. I'm not going to speculate where that leads us just yet, but I will say that I've spent enough years apart from Flick. So the future, right now, has me at his side.

I think hearts everywhere just melted. Thank you, gentlemen. It was a pleasure to speak with you. Best of luck to both of you, but especially to you in your new role with the Guardians, Zander.

Chaos Station by the Numbers

Random facts and figures:

- Zed might have had the nickname Zee if he was written by an American.
- Elias hates snakes.
- Nessa served as a civilian doctor during the early part of the war.
- Qek has a significant video collection…for educational purposes. No, really!
- Felix's favorite sport is basketball.
- Zed's decision to get involved with a married man during his first posting almost ended his career.
- Nessa makes the best cookies in the galaxy.
- Elias is a closet anarchist.
- Felix's birthday is February fifteenth. He hasn't celebrated it in four years and doesn't think Elias knows the date.
- Qek practices her idiom use while the rest of the crew is sleeping. She probably makes use of her *video* collection then too.
- Zed has a not so secret preference for expensive grooming products.
- Humans and ashushk cannot eat one another's food. They can drink one another's booze, though!
- Qek is ninety-two years old, Standard. That's human time. Ashushk days and years are longer than ours, though, so she's younger in Ashushk years, say about forty, which is considered a young adult.
- Elias knows the date of Felix's birthday, he just hasn't figured out how to throw him a party without signing his own death warrant.
- Zed's "equipment" points slightly to the left.

- Felix's "equipment" is longer than Zed's, thus proving the theory skinny little guys are always well hung.
- Qek is only four feet, ten inches tall.
- Felix is the second shortest member of the crew, by an eighth of an inch. As such, he prefers to leave his boots on at all times.
- Nessa has considered buying boots with thicker soles just to taunt Felix.
- Zed is the tallest, but not by much. He's only got an inch or so on Elias.
- Elias is completely and utterly unconcerned by comparisons of height, weight and build.
- The *Chaos* is named for the primeval void from Greek mythology. The space from where the world came into being. Felix picked the name as a way of connecting with Zed, even though he never expected to see him again.
- Felix loves strawberries.
- The project started out with the working title: Space Boys. We didn't actually name the first book "Chaos Station" until we were nearly ready to submit the manuscript.
- The series is named for the first book because Kristen Ashley already had a "Chaos" series.
- It took us about four weeks to write the first book. We had so much fun, we started writing the second book a couple days later.
- Total time between "Chapter One" being written for *Chaos Station* and finding out Carina Press wanted the series: about 5 months.
- We dedicated the first book to the role play characters that inspired us to write the series, Aedan and Iain. Yes, we dedicated a book to fictional people.
- We rewrote the first half of *Lonely Shore* (book 2), during the developmental edit stage.

- The title for *Lonely Shore* comes from the poem "Childe Harold's Pilgrimage" by Lord Byron. The relevant passage is quoted inside the book.
- *Lonely Shore* is dedicated to Zed.
- No one was supposed to die in the first book.
- Someone was always going to die in the second book.
- Our body count rose as we progressed through the series. (Cue evil laughter)
- We rewrote the beginning of *Skip Trace* (book 3) three times.
- The plot of *Skip Trace* changed so significantly during rewrites that we nearly had to change the name of the book.
- *Skip Trace* is dedicated to Felix.
- It took us eight weeks to write *Inversion Point* (book 4). We had no significant rewrites. (Yay!)
- We did have to rename book 4, however. It started out life as *Ghost Ship*. We like the name *Inversion Point* much better.
- *Inversion Point* is dedicated to our husbands.
- *Phase Shift* (book 5) took the most amount of time to write—probably because we were subconsciously putting off the end. (Sad face) Again, we had no significant rewrites. In fact, we didn't even receive an edit letter for our second round!
- We dedicated the last book in the series to our captain, Elias.
- Apparently we like dedicating our books to fictional people!
- The covers of all the books were designed at once, to ensure there was a solid series feel to each. When we saw the towers on the cover for *Phase Shift*, we told the team we'd incorporate them into the book—which wasn't difficult as they certainly fit the theme of the story.
- In order to get a feel for Zed and Felix, and their history together, we wrote back-and-forth scenes in their points of view for two significant periods in their lives before the start of the war. Both were later rewritten as additional stories for readers. "Graduation" is the story of when Felix finally decides to tell Zed he's in love with him. Champion of picking his moment, he chooses the night they graduate Shepard Academy, which is also the last night they'll see

each other for two years. "Reunion" is set four years and a couple of relationships later. This time it's Zed's turn to tell Felix how he feels. He gets a fist to the jaw for his trouble.

- Shepard Academy is named after Alan Shepard, the first American to venture into space. The name is also homage to one of our favorite video game series of all time, *Mass Effect*.
- We have written two other short stories for the boys and plan to write at least one more. They need a honeymoon!
- We've commissioned art for most of the crew and as long as Tami Santarossa continues to enjoy bringing our characters to life, we'll continue asking until we have everyone done.
- All of the titles of the Chaos Station series are metaphorical.
- We have more books planned in the Chaos Station universe, but *Phase Shift* is the final chapter for Zed and Felix. We've tortured them enough.

The CHAOS STATION series:

Chaos Station
Lonely Shore
Skip Trace
Inversion Point
Phase Shift

Visit our website for chapters and excerpts!

http://chaosstation.com

ABOUT THE AUTHORS

Jenn and Kelly met in 2009 through a mutual infatuation with a man who wasn't real. After all but crashing the video game's forums with daily dissection of their obsession, they started writing together, discovered they really liked writing together and began plotting stories in worlds of their own creation.

The CHAOS STATION series aren't the first books they've written together, and they're pretty sure they won't be the last. As long as their so-called smartphones keep making autocorrects that trigger brainstorming sessions, they'll have enough character ideas and plots to keep them writing for years to come.

Connect with Jenn
http://jennburke.com
https://www.facebook.com/jeralibu/
Twitter: @jeralibu

Connect with Kelly
https://kellyjensenwrites.com/
https://www.facebook.com/kellyjensenwrites/
Twitter: @kmkjensen

Made in the USA
Coppell, TX
11 January 2024

27580900R00121